Lock Down Publications and Ca$h Presents

Treacherous YN

Treacherous By Nature

Written By

KHUFU

First Edition 2026

Printed in the United States of America

Lock Down Publications
P.O. Box 944
Stockbridge, GA 30281
www.lockdownpublications.com

Like our page on Facebook: Lock Down Publications
www.facebook.com/lockdownpublications.ldp

Stay Connected with Us!

Text **LOCKDOWN** to 22828 to stay up-to-date with new releases, sneak peaks, contests and more…

Like our page on Facebook:
Lock Down Publications

Join Lock Down Publications/The New Era Reading Group

Visit our website:
www.lockdownpublications.com

Follow us on Instagram:
Lock Down Publications

Email Us: We want to hear from you!

Letter From Khufu

Dear Readers,

I want to thank you for choosing to read *Treacherous YN*. I hope you enjoyed it and if you did, I would love for you to write a review. I'd love to hear what you think. It makes a real difference helping new readers discover one of my books for the first time.

If you wanna keep up to date with my latest releases from LockDown Publications, just go to the website www.LockDownPublications.com or Amazon. Also, I love to hear from readers! You can keep in touch with me through Facebook or IG. Please follow me.

FB: Amos Moss (Big Khufu)
IG: BigKhufu_da_Blazer

Acknowledgements

To the Almighty Creator for giving me this ability to present perspective through a pen. To Ca$h for getting me out there, and a special thank you to the editors and my incredibly supportive fans… you make it all worthwhile! To Tam Bam for being so supportive in my darkest moment. One time for my slimes… Big Rollack type shit! Ola Ken, Mack II, Freeband Gang, Slaughter Gang, Ola Tyson (Python) and shout out to Kream and them A.M.G.s! You already know I gotta salute the city that made me! Fort Pierce, Florida (The City of No Pity!)

Long Live

Stacie, Tayda, Tela, Lanetta, Man Man, Jumpman Krank, Cody, Crazy E

Free Da Real

Killa, Jimmy Reeves, Quinten Bradley, C-Rock, Jermy, Keedy, Scrab, Tre Plus, Pop from Pompano, Coop from D.C.

Quote

"The soul attracts that which it secretly harbors."

Dedication

I dedicate this book to Tammy.

Chapter 1

(Yes Ma'am)

"Khalil! Get'cho ass up and get ready for school!" Ms. Penny yelled, irritated with one of her twin sons. "This my second time comin' in here and yo' ass still in here, laid up, like yo' ass pay bills up in this mothafucka! Kaleb, been dressed and ready waitin' on yo' po- lazy ass! Get the fuck up!" Penny screamed, snatching the cover off of Khalil. Kaleb was Khalil's twin brother. The only distinction between them was their complexion. Kaleb was lighter than Khalil.

"Ma, I ain't got nothin' to wear!" Khalil cried, wiping the crust from his eyes.

"I wouldn't give a fuck! I told yo' ass. If you can afford to buy and smoke weed, you can buy yo' own clothes, mothafucka! Ya ass getting' up outta here this mornin'!" Penny threatened, storming off.

"Bitch," Khalil mumbled up under his breath. Penny didn't know that the weed Khalil was smoking was coming from her boyfriend, Skinny Pimp. Pimp was twenty years old, eight years younger than Penny. He was a young hustler who kept a slew of bitches, dubbing him the name Pimp. He slid in Khalil's room after Penny headed downstairs.

"Say, lil homie. If you don't wanna go to school, just leave the house, and wait till ya mama go to work. Double back when she leave and come home. I'll buy you some clothes later," promised Pimp.

"Nah, I'ma just go to school. Fuck it," Khalil pronounced, getting up to get ready for school.

"Aight, lil homie, catch you later," Pimp retorted, leaving to get his early morning hustle on. Moments later, Kaleb walked in the room with a red and black Polo outfit in his hands.

"Here bra, you can wear this," Kaleb offered, laying the clothes on Khalil's bed.

"I'm good, bra. Fuck it, I'ma just thug it," Khalil proclaimed, yawning while stretching and rubbing his hands through his ear-length dreads.

"You sho'?" Kaleb asked, brushing his head full of deep waves.

"Yeah," Khalil assured, sliding out of bed to put on the same clothes he had on Sunday, the day before. He slipped on an ashy black t-shirt, some black imitation designer jeans, and an old pair of Jumpman sneakers.

"I'll be downstairs waitin' on you, bra," Kaleb stated, before leaving out of the room. Khalil went in the bathroom, threw water on his face, gargled some water, spit in the sink then headed downstairs. When he made it to the bottom of the steps, he saw his mother handing Kaleb some money for school.

"Ma, let me get money for school," Khalil asked.

"Boy, dem krackaz feed you in school. You better get out my face wit' all that," Penny retorted, heading back upstairs. Khalil shook his head in disgust as he watched his mother go up the stairs and disappear. He then opened the front door and headed out, with Kaleb close behind. Khalil and Kaleb were both thirteen, in the eighth grade, and they went to Southport Middle School. Kaleb was suave and popular, while Khalil was more of an introvert. On the way to the bus stop, Khalil pulled out a blunt and sparked it. He inhaled and exhaled while observing the fiends and stray animals roam the streets.

"You wanna hit this shit, Mama's boy?" Khalil asked.

"Yeah right. You know I'on smoke that shit," Kaleb countered.

"You green as fuck," Khalil retorted with a chuckle.

"That peer pressure shit don't work on me, nigga," Kaleb responded unfazed, brushing his hair.

"So, what'chu think, you better than me, kuz you don't smoke?" Khalil asked, blowing smoke from his nose. Kaleb placed the back of his hand on Khalil's chest, forcing him to stop walking and look deep into his eyes.

"Look, bra! I ain't on that shit you on! Nigga, you my brother and I'll die bout 'chu, fool. Fuck, I look like, judging you kuz you smoke weed? Come on wit' all that, bra," Kaleb expressed. Khalil smiled then took another pull from his blunt. He exhaled then responded.

"What'chu call yaself, tryna G-check me?" Khalil askedasked, still smiling as they both started walking again.

"How ever you take it, nigga. You gone pipe down wit' all that Mama's boy shit, too," proclaimed Kaleb.

"Or what, nigga?"

"I'ma get on yo' ass!"

"Imagine that," Khalil stated as they approached the bus stop on 2nd and G.

"Wassup, lil homie?" Skinny Pimp yelled from his smoke gray scat that was parked at the corner opposite their bus stop. Khalil approached Pimp's car while Kaleb remained at the bus stop brushing his hair.

"Wat up?" Khalil retorted, leaning in Pimp's window. He did a quick scan of Pimp's car and noted a shoe box on the passenger floor and three different phones on the passenger seat.

"You wanna roll wit' me?" Pimp asked, putting the finishing touches on a Grabba Leaf that he was rolling.

"Roll wit'chu where?" questioned Khalil, flicking the roach down from his blunt in the street.

"Spinnin' the city and shit… you know, show you what a day like wit' da Pimp," Skinny Pimp asserted, sparking his blunt. Khalil gazed at the statement pieces on Pimp's neck and wrist overtly while ponderous moments ticked by. "You wanna go to school, or you want me to show you how to get some of this shit?" Pimp asked, popping his Cubans and flashing a few bankrolls.

"I'ma just go to school big homie," Khalil declined with a bite of regret painted on his face. Pimp laughed, then took a toke from his blunt.

"Aight, lil homie," Pimp exclaimed, peeling off five twenties and handing it to Khalil. "Let me know when you ready. Grab you some eat at school wit'chu a lil chick or somethin'. I'ma see you when you get home," Pimp proclaimed, starting his engine.

"Bet, that up, my nigga," Khalil replied stuffing the money in his ashy jeans.

"Yeah, yeah," Pimp hollered then pulled off. When Khalil turned around, he noted how crowded the bus stop had gotten and how his brother was gazing at him, brushing his hair.

"What Pimp was hollin' 'bout?" Kaleb asked surrounded by young women.

"He wasn't, really screamin' 'bout nothin'," Khalil brushed off briskly.

"Yeah, I bet," Kaleb retorted with an air of dismissal.

"Heeyyy, Khalil," a tall slim beauty chirped while invading Khalil's personal space. She was slim-thick with mocha skin, and bibulous lips.

"Wassup, Janay," Khalil responded dryly. Janay had a fatal crush on Khalil since the fifth grade, but he didn't see her like that.

"Yeah, heeyyy Khalil," Kaleb clowned with an enormous Kool-Aid smile plastered on his face.

"Fuck you, nigga," spat Khalil.

"Can I have a hug?" Janay cried, poking her lips out.

Khalil reached out and gave her a half hug while she gripped him with both arms like she missed him. "Damn, you smell good," he admitted.

"Dolce &Gabbana," Janay boasted as the school bus pulled up.

"I see you, boy," Kaleb instigated before stepping onto the bus.

Khalil shook his head and stepped on behind him.

"One of y'all lil mothafuckaz, smell like weed! Khalil, I know that's you! You got one moe time to step on my bus, smellin' like that shit! Ya ass won't be getting' on this mothafucka!" threatened the bus driver, Ms. Sermons.

"Yes ma'am!" Khalil yelled. "Need to let a nigga put his dick in yo' old thick ass," he mumbled under his breath before taking the last seat in the back of the bus. Before he could get comfortable, Janay squeezed in next to him.

"You mind if I park all this ass next to you?" she questioned seductively.

Khalil exhaled defeatedly. "Nall, you good," he retorted as the bus pulled off.

"Good," Janay pronounced, slipping her hand into Khalil's ashy jeans and finding his dick.

"Da fuck?" Khalil muttered with a screw face.

"Shhhh…!" she countered, working Khalil's dick proficiently.

"Shhit," he moaned.

"I know," Janay boasted, slipping his now hard dick from his pants and swallowing him whole. She kissed the base of his dick then pulled it from her mouth, making a popping sound with the head of his dick.

"Ffffuck," he moaned again.

"You want me to stop?"

"Fffuck, no," he whispered in pure bliss. Janay laughed.

"I didn't think so," she whispered then proceeded to suck Khalil off like a true porn star. Khalil held his head back, bit his bottom lip, and enjoyed his ride all the way to school.

Chapter 2

(Opp Azz Nigga)

It was near noon when Khalil was walking through the hall, heading to the cafeteria for lunch. He was trailing behind Marcia Morris, a light-skinned beauty with long natural hair and a celestial body. Khalil had been infatuated with her since the sixth grade but never made a pass at her. High off the weed he'd smoked in the restroom during last period, Khalil was feeling himself and said fuck it.

"Wassup Marcia? You wit' me today?" Khalil boldly asked.

Marcia looked back to see who had called her and smiled when she saw that it was Khalil. "Wit'chu where, boy?" she questioned, still smiling, showing her perfectly white teeth and deep dimples.

"Lunch on me? Let a nigga feed you," he proposed, grabbing her hand, forcing her to stop and face him. Marcia did a quick glance at Khalil's apparel, then back to his grim eyes. Even though Khalil's gear wasn't up to par, Marcia found his roughness attractive.

"How you come to school wit' no bookbag?"

"How you walkin' deez hallz, wit' no man?" he countered.

"How you know I'm not headed to him right now?"

"Kuz, you wouldn't still be here, talkin' to me," Khalil pronounced, lifting her hand and placing a tender kiss on it.

"Umm, hmm! So, why you just now sayin' somethin' to me?" she asked, biting her bottom lip. Khalil exhaled before replying.

"You know, you Miss Vogue and shit. All dem niggaz on yo line, I just been waitin' to strike," Khalil explained.

"Ms. Vogue?"

"Yeah, Ms. Popular and shit," Khalil retorted, as they began to walk again. Marcia laughed and continued to smile, elated that Khalil had finally approached her.

"You still shoulda said somethin', that popular shit don't mean nothin' to me," Marcia stated in all seriousness.

"Better late than never, right?"

"I guess," she retorted with a coy giggle.

"So, you eatin' wit me, or nall?" Khalil intoned fervently.

"You sho' yo' lil girlfriend Janay gone approve of that?" Marcia asked, grinning impudently.

"Tsssss…! Here you go. That ain't my lady, where you get that from?" he questioned, his eyebrows raised.

"Word around town," she countered, shrugging her shoulders.

"Yeah, she on me, but that ain't my vibe. I'm smellin' you right nah."

"I hear you," Marcia assured.

"So, we eatin' or what?" Marcia inhaled deeply then exhaled all the while smiling.

"Yeah, let's do it."

* * *

Khalil headed to a table where Marcia was waiting for him and placed four slices of pepperoni pizza, two things of hot wings and two Cokes in front of her, then had a seat next to her.

"You want anything else?" asked Khalil.

"No, this is more than enough. Thank you," Marcia assured, wasting no time on the hot wings.

"Damn, girl!"

"What?"

"You got sauce all on the side of ya face," said Khalil laughing.

"Well, you ain't bring no napkins so whateva."

"Don't trip, come here," Khalil pronounced, using his index finger to wipe the side of her mouth. He then sucked the sauce from his finger.

"Ummm! You did all that, you should of just sucked it off my face," she voiced, taking another bite from a wing, intentionally leaving sauce on her face. Khalil placed his hand under her chin and guided her face closer to his. He then licked the sauce from the side of her face and trailed his tongue to her lips and proceeded to kiss her intensely. Marcia obliged, moaning shamelessly.

"Marcia! What the fuck you doin' wit' this bum ass nigga?" spat a bully-type nigga named Deon. Deon was from the other side of town, technically making him an opp. He was obsessed with Marcia, but she never gave him the time of day. Khalil looked up at Deon and smirked demonically.

"Give me a walk, homie," Khalil insisted calm but threateningly.

"Please do, kuz you really outta pocket right nah," Marcia added, her eyebrows creased.

"How in the fuck I'm outta pocket, when you sittin' here wit' this dirty ass nigga? That ashy ass black t-shirt, wit' them old ass Jumpman's on! Give you a walk? How bout you suck my dick, opp ass nigga!" Deon suggested, using his left hand to pull his dreads from his face to the back of his head. Khalil attempted to rise, but Marcia put her hand on his shoulder.

"Khalil, no," she pleaded.

"It's aight, ma. Enjoy yo' food, I'll pull up later," Khalil promised, rising from the table. "Go 'head, bra. You want her that bad, shid, you can have her," exclaimed Khalil, walking away.

"Khalil!" Marcia yelled.

"Yeah, get from round here, opp ass nigga!" yelled Deon, then focused his attention back on Marcia.

"I can't stand you!"

"Just let me talk to you real quick… damn, Marcia," Deon pleaded.

Before Marcia could contest, Khalil had yanked Deon by his dreads, pulling him to the ground.

"Bitch ass nigga!" Khalil yelled and immediately proceeded to stomp on Deon's face with his old ass Jumpman's.

"Khalil!" Marcia yelled, worried.

Kaleb had just paid for his food when he saw his brother stomping Deon's face in. He dropped his food on the cafeteria floor and rushed to aid Khalil. Kaleb wasted no time kicking Deon in the ribs, cracking a few.

"How you like my Jumpman's nah? Huh, pussy?" Khalil asked, splattering Deon's blood all over his shoes. A crowd formed around the trio and cheered the brothers on. Right before the resource officer and three deans rushed in, Khalil straddled Deon and mashed his face in with wild combinations. Spotting authorities beforehand, Kaleb managed to slip into the crowd while Khalil was discovered atop of Deon, inflicting pain.

The resource officer snatched Khalil up from behind. He managed to slip one more kick to Deon's bloody face before being dragged to the dean's office. Marcia had come down to the dean's office to convey that Dean started it, but her words fell upon death ears. Khalil was suspended for ten days.

* * *

When Kaleb and Khalil entered their apartment, their mother was sitting in the living room on the sofa, smoking a molly joint and sipping from a pint of peach Crown Royal.

The look on her face was vile and villainous, alerting Khalil of the malevolence to come.

"Wassup, Moma?" Khalil pronounced, making his way to the stairs.

"Hey baby," Penny retorted, blowing molly smoke from her nose.

"What up, Moma?" Khalil added.

"Don't 'what up Moma' me, mothafucka! You wanna tell me why yo got them krackaz callin' me 'bout some fuckin' cracked ribs and a broken nose? Huh? You suspended for ten fuckin' days, you lil mothafucka!" she vented.

"Ma, he started wit' me first," Khalil tried to explain.

"Shut the fuck up! go get'cha ass in the mothafuckin' shower! I don't wanna see yo fuckin' face for ten days, you lil fuck up!"

"Moma, it wasn't his fault," Kaleb added.

"Yes, it was! His ass shoulda walked away! I'on know why he just can't be good like you. He gone end up in prison, just like y'all no good ass daddy!" Kaleb and Khalil's father had caught a life sentence for killing a man that he caught in his house with their mother. The thought of his mother praising Kaleb and talking down on him had Khalil in a seething state. He grabbed some clothes and headed to the shower. Khalil had been in the shower for ten minutes with his thoughts circling his consciousness when the shower curtain was snatched open.

"Bitch!" Penny yelled while swinging an extension cord at Khalil's wet body.

"Da fuck! Aye! ma, you trippin," Khalil yelled, jumping and turning his body while covering his dick with both hands.

"Nall-motha-fucka-you-trippin!" Penny retorted as she continued to latch on to Khalil's flesh.

"Aahh! Sshit!" Khalil cried before catching the extension cord from her hand mid-swing. "Gimme this shit!" Khalil spat, snatching the cord from her hands.

"Oh, you gone snatch shit from me? So, you grown nah, lil mothafucka? Get'cha bad ass in yo' room and don't fuckin' come out!" Penny screamed before storming out of the bathroom. Khalil shook his head, threw the cord on the floor, then dried off before getting dressed. When he entered his room, Kaleb was in there waiting for him.

"You aight, bra?" Kaleb asked, concerned.

"Maaan, I'on wanna rap, bra. I'on feel like being fucked wit' so slide, my nigga," Khalil voiced.

"It wouldn't be me if I ain't come and check on you, bra. I'm not the enemy. We family, my nigga. Moma was wrong and I let her know that, too."

"Yeah, I hear you but get the fuck out. I'on feel like people right nah. Respect my mind, BRA!" Khalil enunciated.

"I respect it," Kaleb assured before leaving Khalil's room.

Khalil slammed his door, then opened his closet to put his dirty clothes in the hamper. When he looked up, he saw that his closet was full of designer clothes and shoes.

Da fuck? he thought until his mind replayed what Skinny Pimp had told him earlier that day. Khalil smiled, then lay in his bed pondering his next move.

Chapter 3
(Don't Trip)

It was 6:40 am when Penny had entered Khalil's room and found him awake, gazing at the ceiling. He had only received two hours of sleep due to his thoughts running rampant. For the life of him, Khalil couldn't fathom the reason why his mother treated him differently from his brother, if they were twins.

"Khalil! I'm headed to work! I want this house clean, top to bottom, and stay yo' ass in this house! Ain't no going outside! You hear me?" Penny asked irritably.

"Yeah!" Khalil assured, still gazing at the ceiling, never looking his mother's way.

"Good," she retorted, slamming his door before leaving to go to work. Moments later, Kaleb walked in dressed for school.

"Top of the mornin, bra. I'm headed to school. You good?" Khlil glanced at Kaleb then diverted his attention back to the ceiling.

"Yeah, nigga, I'm good," Khalil replied.

"Aight. Fuck wit'chu when I get back," Kaleb retorted, then left the room. Thirty ponderous minutes ticked by and Khalil was still gazing at the ceiling when his room door flung open.

"Wassup, lil nigga!" When Khalil turned to look, he noticed Skinny Pimp standing in his doorway, smiling with all thirty-two gold teeth gleaming. Khalil couldn't help smiling himself.

"What up, Pimp?" Khalil retorted, sitting up.

"You already know what time it is! A day in the life of Pimp, lil nigga. You seen yo' closet?"

"Yeah man, thank you," Khalil exclaimed.

"Yeah, yeah. Don't sweat that lil shit. Get dressed and meet me in the scat. Hurry up, too," Pimp pronounced, leaving Khalil's room. Khalil jumped in the shower for five minutes then got dipped in a pair of thirteen-hundred-dollar Gallery Dept. fatigue pants, a red Balenciaga t-shirt, and a pair of all-red high-top Jordan 11's. When he made it to Pimp's passenger seat, he was smoking Obama Runts and talking on his phone.

"Man, I'on give no fucks bout-cha billz, ya kids, or none of that shit! Da fuck that shit got to do wit' my mothafuckin' money, nigga?" Pimp snapped, passing Khalil the blunt. "When I pull up, have my paper or it's *dhat*!" Click! Pimp hung the phone up then put the car in reverse. "Wat up, lil nigga, you aight?"

"Yeah, I'm good."

"Right then, we rollin, baby. Look in the glove box and roll that shit up. You know how to roll, right?" Pimp asked.

Khalil snuffled a laugh before opening the glove box. When he grabbed the cigars and weed, he locked eyes on a beautiful SR 22 Ruger with an ambidextrous safety and fell in love instantly. Pimp peeped game and smirked.

"You like what'chu see?" Pimp asked a rhetorical question.

"Hell yeah!" Khalil retorted, excitement dripping from his voice.

"Shid, pick it up." Khalil looked at Pimp to see if he was serious. Pimp affirmed it with a head nod and a golden smile. Khalil grabbed the pistol then examined its beauty. The hairs stood on Khalil's arms and neck as the power of death rested in his hands.

"You ever used one of them before?" Khalil shook his head no, never taking his eyes off the gun. Pimp chuckled. "Don't trip, you wit' the Pimp. Slide it in ya pocket, lil nigga, that's yours. Roll that gas up, too," Pimp insisted, making a call on his phone.

Khalil gazed at Pimp in an eager manner then did what he was told. Being frowned upon by his mother for as long as he could remember, Khalil couldn't fathom why Pimp was treating him like a human instead of a mistake. Whatever the reason… Khalil embraced it.

* * *

Khalil and Erica had been fucking for three hours straight. The coke that she sprinkled on Khalil's dick had him numb and performing his greatest. He had both of her legs pinned to the mattress, while the sound of his pelvis slapping against her vagina echoed throughout the room and hallway. He was putting in so much work that the sweat from his face dripped into Erica's. She was so much of a freak that she opened her mouth and allowed the sweat to drip in her mouth.

"Ummmmmm… Yessss! Give it to me, baby! Right there, right there, don't you dare stop fuckin' this wet pussy!" Erica cried, cumming for the twentieth time.

"Shhhhhittt! This pussy so fuckin' good!" Khalil admitted as the sound of her wetness serenaded the room. Smack! Smack! Smack! Smack! Smack! Smack! Smack! The sound of their flesh colliding continued to echo throughout the house.

"Spit in my mouth, daddy!"

"Huh?" Khalil asked, still dropping meat deep off in Erica's love nest.

"Spit in my fuckin' mouth! Do it now!" she begged. Khalil coughed up a loogie and dropped it into Erica's mouth. Watching her swallow it caused Khalil's dick to grow hard as obsidian stone. Erica's eyes rolled to the back of her head, followed by an awkward squawk.

"Aaaahhhaaaa!!!" Erica screamed as she began to squirt all over Khalil's mid-section.

"Da fuck?" Khalil yelled, snatching out of her and moving to the side. He watched her wetness spray across the room in bewilderment. She shook violently and cried out to her creator solemnly. When her orgasm began to subside, Khalil snapped.

"Bitch! I know you ain't jus pissed on me!"

"SSSS…Whoooo, shhit!" she moaned while the shaking had seemed to stop. "No baby, I squirted. You was hitting my spot, and that's what happens when you do."

Khalil rubbed his chin with his left hand while his right arm was folded across his chest. He still didn't quite understand. Erica crawled out of bed and grabbed Khalil by the hand. "Why did you call me a bitch, baby?" Khalil remained silent with a screw face. "Come on daddy, let's go take a shower," she suggested, pulling Khalil by the hand.

Chapter 4

(That's A Good Boy)

Three hours later, Pimp and Khalil were in Brighton on a Seminole Indian reservation, pulling into one of his long-time customer's property by the name of Erica Oceola. He met her in the Hard Rock Casino a year ago and they'd been friends with benefits ever since. In Fort Pierce, Pimp sold ounces for a thousand dollars, but in Brighton he sold Erica four ounces for six thousand, at fifteen hundred a piece. She didn't mind paying the extra two thousand for the trafficking because coke on the reservation was scarce.

"Where we at?" Khalil asked, surveying his surroundings.

"Indian reservation. Step out, and brang ya pistol," Pimp retorted, grabbing a brown bag and lighting a blunt before stepping out. Khalil did as he was told.

He noticed that four-wheelers, dirt bikes, mud trucks, and foreigns littered the property.

"Damn," Khalil muttered loud enough for Pimp to hear.

"Wassup, you fuckin' wit' it?" Pimp asked, smiling.

"Hell yeah," Khalil admitted. At the same time, an Indian beauty exited the enormous home.

"Hey, Pimp," Erica greeted, her mouth full of gold teeth and deep dimples complimenting each other. Khalil noted that she was a little heavy-set, but beautiful as ever, dipped in diamonds and gold.

"Wassup, E?" Pimp retorted, hugging her tenderly.

"You already know. I'm ready to get down," exclaimed Erica, diverting her attention towards Khalil.

"I got'chu. This my lil homie, Khalil. Khalil, this Erica."

"How you doin, handsome?" Erica asked, holding her hand out.

"I'm good," Khalil replied, shaking her hand.

"Nice to meet'chu, Khalil. Y'all wanna come inside?"

"Nah, we gone be 'round back. Here," Pimp asserted, handing her a brown paper bag. In return, Erica handed Pimp an envelope, then headed back inside.

"Come on," Pimp said as he headed towards the back of the house. Khalil followed Pimp and became enthralled at what laid before him. Under an enormous hut sat an above-ground Jacuzzi, pool tables, Armani sofas, a bar with a seventy-five-inch flat screen, and a table with a fireplace in the center of it.

"Damn," Khalil muttered as they pushed past the hut and further into the backyard. Khalil almost lost his mind when he found himself standing in front of a glass tank with a twelve-foot alligator trapped inside.

"Man, this shit here crazy," pronounced Khalil with a lopsided grin.

"Yeah, real swamp life shit," Pimp added, pushing past the tank.

"Come on, lil nigga," Pimp ordered. Khalil followed close behind until they reached what seemed to be some sort of shooting range.

"What's this?"

"Look, homie. You know where you from. Becoming a steppa is inevitable. You gone be a victim or you gone be the one victimizing. Judging by yo' suspension from school, I see you standin' on bidness, but what happens when you run into the nigga you demonstrated on in the street?"

"Shid… demonstrate again," Khalil replied firmly.

"Yeah, I hear you, but niggaz don't fight no moe. You got off the first time cause you was in school. Tell me, where the nigga from?"

"He from 13th," Khalil answered. Pimp shook his head from left to right.

"Them niggaz is killaz, from the old heads to the lil niggaz. You can't play wit' dem niggaz over there. Pull ya pistol out," demanded Pimp. Khalil did as he was told.

"Aight, look. Hold that mothafucka wit' two hands and line yo' target up wit' the sight on top of ya gun." Khalil aimed at the target, which was a picture of a turkey. "Exhale and pull the trigger." Khalil exhaled and squeezed off a shot, hitting the turkey in the stomach.

"Good shot, lil ni—" Boc! Boc! Boc! Boc! Khalil squeezed off four more shots, hitting the target in the neck and face. Pimp looked at the target then back at Khalil. He then smiled a devilish one. "Okay, Bass Reeves!" Pimp clowned, calling Khalil the name of the first known cowboy who was also black. Khalil examined the pistol, loving the smell of gun smoke and the power it possessed.

"Y'all okay back here?" Erica asked rubbing her nose.

"Yeah, we Gucci," Pimp assured.

"How about you, Khalil?" Khalil shook his head up and down. Pimp made his way over to Erica and whispered in her ear.

"You know I got'chu, Pimp," Erica exclaimed, smiling.

"Aye, Khalil, come on. You did good, nah let's go have us a drink," Pimp pronounced then headed to the bar.

When they reached the bar, Pimp poured three shots of Don Julio.

"Have you ever drank before?" Erica questioned.

"No," Khalil responded.

"Just take it to the head," she instructed.

"Raise ya glasses," Pimp ordered. Everybody raised their glasses.

Khalil's dick head. Erica placed the tip of his dick in her mouth, sucked only the head for a few moments, then gradually bobbed all of him in and out of her mouth artistically.

"Ssss…haaah!" Khalil cried, gripping the sofa for dear life.

Khalil heard Pimp chuckle but couldn't care less. The numbing warm sensation that Erica was administering was foreign, but blissfully amazing.

"Ummm… huh!" Erica moaned, popping Khalil's dick from her mouth. She then climbed atop of him, slid her lace panties to the side and slipped his throbbing dick into her wetness.

"Oooole… ssshit!" Khalil cried, looking Erica deep in her eyes. Khalil had never felt anything more ecstatic.

"I know, baby," Erica boasted, sitting down on his impressive size. She allowed him to marinate inside her while grabbing the sandwich bag.

"You trust me?" Erica asked, sticking her nail in the bag and placing it under Khalil's right nostril. Khalil moved his head to the side dismissively. Erica lifted herself and slid back down on his dick.

"Aaah…shit! Yeah! Yeah, I trust you." Erica smiled, then placed the coke under his nostril. Khalil sniffed the coke from her nail.

"That's a good boy," Erica chortled, placing another bump of coke under his other nostril. Khalil obliged without protest. He relaxed and fell into a state of euphoria.

"Mama gone take good care of you," Erica assured, tucking the bag in her breasts and gripping the back of the sofa for the rodeo show she was about to give Khalil.

Chapter 5
(Bitch Ass Nigga)

It was 3:45 pm when Pimp pulled into the driveway of Penny's apartment and put his scat in park. He gazed at Khalil for a moment before speaking. "Wassup, you aight?" Pimp asked.

"Yeah, I'm good," replied Khalil, using his index finger and thumb to swipe his nose.

"You wit' me tomorrow or what?" Pimp asked, putting flame to his blunt.

"Hell yeah, I'm wit'chu, big homie." Pimp nodded his head back and forth. "Pimp, who is Erica to you?" Pimp passed Khalil the blunt.

"My homegirl and bidness partner. Why, you like her?" Khalil smirked, hit the blunt, then passed it back to Pimp. "Listen lil homie, Erica cool and all that, but that's where you keep it wit' her. She not the kind you fall in love wit', understand?" Khalil nodded his head in understanding. "Always remember, pussy is just temporary pleasure. Don't get wrapped up in that love shit. Love make a nigga weak! It's always about money and standin' on bidness! Don't ever let a mothafucka play wit'chu, you demonstrate and smush his ass! Respect is a must! Understand?"

"I understand, big homie," Khalil assured. Pimp observed Khalil's body language then stuck his hand in his pocket.

"Here," Pimp muttered, handing Khalil three hundred dollars. He then reached under his seat for a shoe box and pulled Khalil a eightball of coke from it.

"Don't tell yo' brother or yo' Moma bout'chu hangin' wit' me, and don't let her see you snort this shit. Keep everything close to ya chest. Aight?" Khalil nodded his head in agreement.

"Alright, big homie," Khalil responded, dappin' Pimp up.

"I'll be here in the morning. Here," Pimp exclaimed, handing Khalil one of his phones. "You can have this phone. This was my hoe phone. Don't pay no attention to 'em when they call. Make sho' you ready in the morning."

"Right, Pimp. Man, I appreciate 'chu," Khalil pronounced before hopping out of the whip and heading inside.

* * *

Khalil was in his room hyped up on coke and playing with his pistol when he heard his mother enter the apartment. He slid the gun under his pillow as the sound of Penny making her way up the steps echoed throughout the apartment.

"Khalil! Why the fuck this house ain't clean?" Penny yelled before opening his room door. "You hear me talkin' to you boy?" Khalil's expression was an irritated one.

"Maan! Shut up and get out!" Khalil shot back.

"Boy! I'll knock…" Penny's words were cut short when she saw the one-hundred-dollar bill he was handing her. She quickly snatched the money from Khalil's hand and tucked it in her bra.

"Where the hell you get this from? So, you sellin' dope nah?"

"NO! Now, please get out!" Khalil warned, standing to his feet.

"Watch yo' fuckin' mouth! And, you still gotta clean this house up," Penny proclaimed, leaving his room and slamming the door.

"Yeah, the fuck right. Better get Kaleb to do that shit," Khalil mumbled, then took another bump of coke. Right when the events of the day started to replay in his mind the phone that Pimp had given him rang. When he picked it up, he noted that it was Erica calling. Pimp's words about Erica replayed in his mental. Also, Pimp told Khalil not to answer the phone, but he did anyway.

"Hello?" he answered.

"Hello, who is this?" Erica asked before making a sniffing sound.

"Khalil."

"Oh, hey, baby. How you feelin'?"

"I'm good, wassup wit-chu?"

"You already know. I'm just out here, relaxing. Is Pimp around?" Erica asked, followed by more sniffing sounds.

"Nawl, he ain't around."

"Damn. Okay. I wish you could have stayed a little longer. You'd love it out here," she pronounced.

"I know. It's so peaceful out there," he added.

"Did you enjoy yourself?"

"Yeah."

"Hell yeah!" Khalil retorted quickly. Erica laughed.

"I enjoyed you too, baby," Erica admitted.

"I'll let Pimp know you called," Khalil proclaimed.

"No need. I'll talk to you later, okay handsome?"

"Fasho." Click! When the call was over, Kaleb opened Khalil's door and entered.

"Wassup, bra?" Kaleb greeted.

"Nigga, knock on my shit next time!" Khalil barked.

"Whateva, nigga! Here," Kaleb replied handing Khalil a piece of paper.

"Fuck is this?"

"Marcia said call her ASAP!" Kaleb informed him, smiling.

"Oh yeah?"

"Yeah. And I seen the nigga Deon today."

"What'chu mean? He supposed to be suspended," Khalil snapped.

"I'on know, bra, I guess not. He told me to tell you, he ain't got no smoke wit-chu," Kaleb stated.

"Nigga what? You talkin' to this bitch ass nigga?"

"Just tellin' you what he said, bra."

"Maan, you was suppose to crush that nigga! Get'cha soft ass out my room, my nigga!" Khalil barked with murder in his eyes. Kaleb shook his head from side to side, then left Khalil's room.

"Bitch ass nigga," Khalil mumbled, then grabbed his phone to call Marcia.

Chapter 6

(You Know What It Is)

The rooster in the Jamaican's yard next door started crowing beautifully, waking up everyone in his radius.

"You heard that?" Khalil asked Marcia. She laughed before replying.

"Yeah, they crowing over here, too. You know my daddy Jamaican."

"Oooww, I got me a lil Jamaican baby?" Khalil clowned. Marcia chuckled again.

"And do! What'chu gone do 'bout Janay?" Marcia asked.

"Stop playin' wit' me, fa I pull up and make ya daddy wanna kill me," Khalil pronounced.

"Shid, pull up. my daddy cool."

"We been on the phone all night. You still goin' to school?" he questioned.

"No. I'm finna go to sleep, unless you finna pull up," Marcia retorted, yawning and stretching.

"I gotta get up and go handle somethin', but I might pull up later," Khalil proclaimed.

"I'll be here," she assured.

"Aight, new bae. Sleep peacefully." Marcia smiled.

"Okay, love." Click! Penny stuck her head inside Khalil's room.

"Boy, I'm gone to work! Don't have nobody in my house and make sho' this house clean!" Penny slammed the door, not giving him time to respond.

"Whateva man," Khalil whispered, taking a bump of coke in each nostril. The moment he was done, Kaleb knocked twice before entering.

"I'm gone to school, bra. See you when you get back," Kaleb said easily.

"Maan, you ain't gotta do all that! Shut my door, and take ya ass to school, opp lover!" Khalil dismissed him with a sound of disgust.

"Nigga, you trippin'!" Kaleb responded, closing the door behind him.

"Stupid ass nigga," Khalil sneered. he got up and decided to take a shower.

Ten minutes into the shower, there was a knock at the door.

"Yeah!"

"Tighten up, nigga! You know that the lick read!" Pimp yelled.

"Be out in a minute!" Khalil yelled. Five minutes later, he was out of the shower getting dressed. He got dripped in a black Celine sweatsuit and a pair of Dior Air Jordan Hi-Tops, black and white. He sprayed the Creed that Pimp bought for him, grabbed his pistol and headed out. When he hopped in the whip, Pimp was on the phone conducting business. He lowered the phone for a second to get at Khalil.

"Roll up," Pimp whispered, then continued his conversation. Khalil grabbed the Backwoods and zaza from the console and proceeded to twist up.

"So, you got my money, and you want a nine? Yeah, aight. Meet me off of Juanita, behind the plaza at the basketball court in an hour. One hour, nigga!" Click! Pimp hung the phone up.

"Wassup, lil homie? You aight? How you slept?" Pimp asked, reaching for the blunt. "Roll yo' own spliff. I need one to the head," he stated, putting flame to it.

"Aight. I ain't get no sleep, but I'm good," Khalil asserted.

"All night flight, huh?" Pimp inquired, pulling off.

"I was vibin' wit' this lil baby from school."

"Oh yeah?" Pimp asked. Khalil nodded his head.

"Speakin' of lil babies. Didn't I tell you not to answer the phone if one of my hoes called?" Khalil instantly felt as if he was having a sucka attack for disappointing Pimp.

"I… I ain't—"

"Relax, lil homie. We good," Pimp assured. "You like Erica?" Khalil nodded his head.

"Yeah, Erica cool," Khalil admitted, putting flame to his blunt.

"You know, I told her to call you, and why. She coulda told me, 'No Pimp, I'm not doin' that,' and I would of respected it. But she went along wit' it. What if I wanted to line you up? She woulda did it, after givin' you the pussy and everything. You my lil homie, so I gotta pull yo' coat on this type shit. Be careful who you give ya trust to… niggaz and bitches! Erica had some good pussy?" Pimp asked. Khalil nodded his head yes.

"Always remember… Good pussy ain't shit compared to loyal pussy. You hear me?"

"I hear you, big homie," Khalil assured. Erica had just left a bad taste in his mouth.

"And don't be mad at Erica. That'll just be a waste of energy."

"Fasho," Khalil retorted.

"One-hunnid," Pimp pronounced, dapping Khalil up. "Listen, you wanna make some money right quick?"

"Hell yeah!" Khalil shot back briskly. Pimp chuckled.

"Aight, I got'cha."

* * *

Pimp made a left on Juanita and turned down a dirt road. After a few yards up, he pulled to the right and parked in front of the desolate basketball court next to Trick's 2024 Mustang. Trick got out of his whip and hopped in the passenger's seat of Pimp's scat.

"Wassup, my guy?" Trick greeted with a 14k smile.

"Cut the small talk. Where my money?" Pimp inquired in a not-so-subtle way.

"Relax, killa, I got it right here," Trick assured, reaching in his pockets for the money. "You got the work?"

"Yeah, I got it. Count that money up, though."

"You want me to count it?" Trick asked dubiously.

"All eighteen bands," Pimp added. Trick shook his head and began to count up. Pimp turned the music up and let the sounds of Kevin Gates' "M.A.T.A." galvanize the atmosphere.

"Make Amerika trap again / Make Amerika trap again
Make Amerika trap again / Make Amerika trap again…"

Trick bobbed his head to the music while counting the money. He never saw or heard Pimp pop the trunk. Khalil climbed out of the trunk and crept his way to the passenger side of the scat. Pimp turned the music down so he could hear and see how Khalil performed.

"You know what it is," Khalil threatened, placing the barrel on Trick's temple with brute force. A palpable sense of fear fan throughout Trick's body as it appeared that Khalil had materialized from out of nowhere.

"Ooh, sshit! Don't kill me! You can have this shit!" Trick pleaded, handing the money to Khalil slowly. Khalil took the money.

"Nigga, put'cha hands on ya head," demanded Khalil. Once his hands were placed on his head, Khalil opened the door.

“Step out and keep ya hands on ya head!” Pimp was smiling in awe.

“Don’t kill me young blood,” Trick cried, trembling.

“Maan, turn around, walk to yo’ shit, get in and leave,” Khalil ordered.

“I got’cha, youngsta. Don’t shoot me, please,” Trick whined, turning to get in his truck.

Boc! Trick dropped dead on the side of his truck. Khalil walked up and stood over him.

Boc! Boc! Khalil gazed down at the man who had fallen to his knees while his upper body slumped forward awkwardly.

“Tighten up!” Pimp called out, snapping Khalil out of a daze. Khalil walked to the car and hopped in. Pimp pulled off and got ghost.

Chapter 7

(Nearest Green)

Pimp occasionally glanced at Khalil from the driver's seat, noting his vibe after his first murder… silent and stoic. He knew Khalil was a killer. The moment had presented itself to bring it out of him, and he executed it prodigiously.

"You aight?" Pimp asked. Khalil nodded his head yes, then reached for a blunt to roll.

"Listen lil homie, killin' a nigga don't make you a man. The reason you did it, and how you deal wit' it afterwards do. A man is made or unmade by himself, you hear me?" asked Pimp.

"I hear you," Khalil assured, sparking a blunt.

"Don't ever put nobody in ya bidness. A silent tongue never betrays its owner," Pimp philosophized, pulling into the driveway of a home on Mayflower Street known as Haitian territory. Pimp killed the engine.

"Get out, and step inside wit' me," he told Khalil. Khalil stepped out with Pimp and followed him inside. Khalil noted the red velvet drapes with matching sofas. His feet sank into the soft fluffy black carpet as he viewed photos of Nipsey Hustle, and Nearest Green on the walls.

“Who that?” Khalil asked, pointing at the photo of Nearest Green.

“That’s Nearest Green. He the one who made all the whiskey for Jack Daniels,” informed Pimp. Khalil recognized the name from his mother’s bottles.

“A black man?”

“Yeah. They tried to hide it, but a black woman named Fawn Weaver exposed it. She even created a bottle of whiskey with his name on it, and nah she a billionaire. All them bottles over there on that bar got Nearest Green on them. You can help yaself, homie.”

“Who stay here?”

“This my spot,” Pimp replied, then headed to a room in the back.

“His spot?” Khalil whispered, his eyebrows furrowed as he made his way to the bar. He removed a sack of coke and took a bump in each nostril. Khalil’s thoughts were all over the place as he poured a shot of whiskey and downed it. Moments later, Pimp returned with a baby Glock .40 in his hand.

“Let me get that Ruger up off you,” Pimp insisted. Khalil gazed at Pimp a few seconds, then reached at his hip and gave him the pistol. In return, Pimp gave Khalil the Glock .40.

“This yo’ new banga, it’s a Glock .40 wit’ a green beam on it. I’ma get rid of this one. You gotta body on it, can’t move around wit this shit.” Khalil nodded his head in understanding while taking the .40.

“Let me ask you somethin’,” Khalil asserted.

“Wassup wit’ it?”

“Why my Moma don’t live here wit’chu?”

“Shid, to be honest,” Pimp said, pouring him a shot, “me and yo’ Moma got our own thang goin’ on. She do her, I do me. I know you might not wanna hear this, but yo’ Moma on molly. I got too much goin’ on over here, ya feel me?” Pimp explained.

"Trust me, I understand big homie," Khalil assured.

"Fasho! That's why I fuck wit'chu."

"I fuck wit'chu too, Pimp." Pimp chuckled.

"Listen. You know what crack is?" asked Pimp.

"Yeah. Never seen it in person, but I seen it on YouTube and how it fucked up our hood," Khalil enunciated.

"Don't 'cha eva smoke that shit! You hear me?"

"I know better than that, Pimp." Pimp nodded his head in approval.

"Look, I'm finna show you how to cook and sell this shit in case you eva wanna jump in this dope game. Aight?"

"Let's do it," Khalil retorted eagerly.

* * *

Khalil had fucked the dope up the first time he tried to cook it, but Pimp melted it back down and made him try it again. Khalil nailed it, dropping twenty-eight grams and bringing back twenty-six.

"Aight, you official nah. Knowin' how to cook is key. Niggaz can't fuck you over, nah," Pimp lectured.

"I appreciate 'chu, forreal," Khalil proclaimed.

"You know the vibe. Let roll out," Pimp suggested.

"I'm following you," Khalil retorted, following Pimp out the door. They both jumped in the whip and crept up Mayflower Street, with Pimp behind the wheel.

"Aye, wassup wit' that lil chick you was on the phone wit' all night?" Pimp asked, while scoping a house down the block from his that was having a lot of motion.

"She cool, why wassup?" Khalil replied.

"You wanna go see her?" Khalil nodded his head yes with a closed lipped smile. Pimp chuckled.

"Call her and see if she woke," Pimp remarked while looking in his rearview mirror. Khalil pulled out his phone and dialed Marcia's number.

* * *

Pimp made a left on 16th Street and Canal then turned into a yellow house that was the last one on that street. When they pulled into the yard, Marcia was sitting on the porch in a red pajama set.

"Go 'head, lil homie, I'll be right here," Pimp stated, putting flame to a blunt. Khalil hopped out with his panache on overdrive. Marcia was instantly smitten by his appearance and couldn't stop smiling.

"Good mornin', gorgeous," Khalil greeted, smiling himself. Marcia stood and wrapped her arms around his neck.

"Morning," Marcia replied. "Damn, you smell good," she admitted.

Khalil wrapped his arms around her and squeezed both of her well-proportioned ass cheeks.

"Creed," Khalil remarked. "Damn, you so soft," he added, kissing her on the lips. Marcia giggled.

"I get it from my Moma."

"Where she at, so I can thank her?" Khalil shot back.

"You so silly," she retorted, unwrapping her arms from around him and taking a step back to look at him from head to toe.

"Wassup?" Khalil questioned.

"Where you going, looking this good at ten o'clock in the morning?"

"Shit, I came to see you," he shot back smoothly.

"Umm-hmm! What'chu into Khalil?" she pried, folding her arms while standing pigeon toed.

"I ain't on nothin'. My moma boyfriend be lookin' out for me."

"That's him in the car?"

"Yeah," Khalil retorted. Marcia waved at Pimp, who in return, threw his index finger up. Marcia cleared her throat.

"So, what's that on yo' shoes?" she irresistibly pointed out.

Khalil glanced at his shoes and saw the blood splattered on them. Before he could reply, the front door of the house opened and a man in his early twenties stepped out and approached the two.

"Who the fuck is this nigga?" The man who snapped had a mouth full of gold teeth and a well-toned build.

"Nigga, what?" Khalil asked, snatching his .40 from his sweats.

Marcia's eyes widened. She then grabbed Khalil's arm at the same time that Pimp hopped out of his car.

"What'chu hollin' 'bout?" Pimp inquired, approaching with his gun drawn.

"No, wait! This is my brother! Y'all don't pay him no attention! Kasper, take yo' stupid ass in the house!" she snapped.

"You got niggaz in the yard wit' guns early in the mornin'! I'm tellin' Moma," Kasper cried, making his way back in the house.

"I'm sorry about that, y'all," Marcia apologized.

"It's all good," Khalil assured, making his way to the car. Marcia followed him closely.

"Can I have a hug?" she asked. Khalil gave her a hug, but his mind was on her brother. He had wished that Kasper was no relation to her, so he could've shed blood.

"You gone call me?"

"Yeah," Khalil said, braking away from her grasp and getting into the car. Marcia stood in her driveway with her arms folded and watched Khalil and Pimp fade away.

"So, you was gone kill fool in front of her?" Pimp questioned.

"No question," Khalil responded with a smug expression on his face.

"Listen, I know you done got'cha first taste of blood, but'chu gotta move strategically wit' the murda game," Pimp expressed.

"Strategically?" Khalil questioned.

"Yeah, you gotta plot and plan shit. Be militant, lil bra, 'cause you can't afford to leave witnesses on the scene. That's a life sentence. You hear me?"

"Yeah, I understand, Pimp."

"Overstand! We don't understand shit, we overstand it." Khalil nodded his head in overstanding.

"I'ma take care of you, lil nigga… I promise!" Khalil gazed at Pimp in adulation. "You know how to drive?" Pimp asked. Khalil shook his head no. "You gone learn today!" Pimp assured.

Chapter 8

(Rock You to Sleep)

Daylight was beginning to fade when Khalil pulled into his mother's driveway. Pimp had been schooling him on how to drive all day and to Pimp's surprise, Khalil nearly had it down to a science.

"You catch on quick, lil homie. I like that bout'chu," Pimp stated, grinning with ill-suppressed satisfaction.

"Sho' me somethin' one time, I'ma perfect it," Khalil added. Pimp nodded his head in approval, while goin' in his pocket to pull out a bankroll. He counted out five bands, then reached under his seat and grabbed three ounces.

"Look here, this three racks and three ounces. You can piss away the coke puttin' it up ya nose, or you can sell the shit, and power up. If I was you, I'd get right and get the fuck out the projects. Whateva you choose to do, I'm wit'chu," Pimp exclaimed genuinely with an edge in his tone that cut across Khalil's consciousness.

"I appreciate 'chu, and I hear you," Khalil retorted accepting what Pimp had blessed him with.

"Boy! What the hell you doin' behind the wheel? Better yet, what the fuck you doin' outta this fuckin' house?" Penny yelled, approaching the car. Khalil tucked the dope, pulled two hundred from his bankroll and quickly held the money out the window.

"Here!" he barked, agitated. Penny's words were cut short when she spotted the money. She snatched the two bills then turned around, heading back inside. Before she reached the door, she turned around.

"Pimp, you gone come in and spend some time with me?" Penny asked with pleading eyes.

"Yeah, I'll be in there," Pimp replied, waving his hand for her to go inside.

"Okay!" When she entered the apartment, Kaleb was coming out. He approached Khalil's side of the vehicle.

"Wassup bra?" Kaleb greeted, checking the temperature to see if his brother was still mad at him.

"Phsssss!" Khalil muttered, waving Kaleb off. "Aye, Pimp, I'm gone," Khalil remarked.

"Aight, I'ma get up wit'chu in the mornin', lil homie," Pimp declared.

"Yeah," Khalil responded, before exiting the vehicle and entering the apartment. Kaleb made his way into the passenger's seat.

"What that be 'bout?" Pimp inquired. Kaleb drew in a deep breath then exhaled loudly.

"He mad at me for talkin' to the nigga we jumped at school," Kaleb pronounced, shaking his head.

"You know you outta pocket, homie. What'chu and buddy got to talk about? he the opps," Pimp questioned, consumed with curiosity. Kaleb collected himself before resuming in an even voice.

"The nigga name is Deon. Deon approached me in school and told me that he didn't want no smoke. He told me to tell

Khalil the same. I told Khalil, nah he mad at me on some 'I'm talkin' to the opps' type shit," Kaleb explained.

"Listen. Don't eva let a nigga rock you to sleep. Y'all put hands and feet on a nigga from the other side. You really think he don't want no smoke?" Pimp explained. Kaleb took in all that Pimp was saying.

"I hear you," Kaled asserted.

"Just stay on point, lil homie. You aight? You need somethin'?" Pimp asked.

"Yeah. I was gone ask you if you could help me get in the Pop Warner League."

"Fasho. How much is it?" Pimp inquired, pulling two hundred from a bankroll and handing it to Kaleb. Kaleb's smile lit up with gratitude.

"That'll do. Thank you, Pimp!" Kaleb pronounced, dapping Pimp up.

"No problem, but do me a favor?" Pimp asked.

"Wassup?"

"Tell yo' moma I'll be back. I gotta handle somethin'," Pimp stated.

"Bet."

Chapter 9

(Killa)

The next morning, when Kaleb went to Khalil's room to let him know that he was headed to school, he found that Khalil was already gone. After checking the entire apartment, Kaleb said goodbye to his mother, then headed to the bus stop. On the way to his bus stop, Kaleb noticed a crowd surrounding someone on the opposite side of his bus stop. The closer he got, the more he realized that the crowd of people were dope fiends. When they scattered, he was caught off guard by Khalil's presence.

"Khalil?" Kaleb asked, approaching. Khalil glanced at Kaleb then back at the money he was counting. Kaleb noted how clean Khalil was, dipped in Amiri and a pair of cocaine-white Forces.

"Damn, you clean as hell! Don't't'chu got like eight days left on suspension? What'chu doin up here?" Kaleb pried.

"What the fuck it look like, nigga? I'm getting money! The fuck you sweatin' me for? Don't't'chu gotta opp nigga to go hang wit? Get the fuck out my face… Moma's boy,"

Khalil snapped, drawing attention from the others at the bus stop.

"Bra, you trippin'! I love you, but don't come at me like that… farreal, my nigga," Kaleb retorted, pleading with his eyes.

"Or what, nigga?" Khalil responded, biting his bottom lip.

"Heeyy, Khalil," Janay sang, approaching and wrapping her arms around Khalil. Her good energy and fragrance changed his mood. He hugged her back.

"Wassup Janay, you miss me?"

"Do I? You lookin' and smellin' good! Umm! Let's go on the side of the house, I wanna eat that dick up," she cried. Khalil laughed at how brazen she was. Right when he was considering it, Pimp pulled up.

"I'ma get wit'chu later, Janay. I gotta go," Khalil pronounced, kissing her on the forehead and hopping in the whip with Pimp.

"Bra, let me talk to you," Kaleb pleaded. Pimp looked over at Khalil.

"Yo' brother wanna holla at'chu, lil homie." Khalil waved him off.

"I'll catch'em later. Let's roll, big homie," Khalil asserted, grabbing cigars and weed from the console to twist up.

"He gone get wit'chu later, lil homie," Pimp told Kaleb. Kaleb nodded his head then walked off disappointed. Pimp blew the horn then pulled off.

"Wassup, big homie, what the lick read?" Khalil asked, putting the finishing touch-ups on the blunt.

"I got somethin' cookin', just chill."

"Fasho," Khalil retorted, sparking his blunt. Pimp took a moment to evaluate Khalil. He was small in stature, but not in heart and was resolute on becoming somebody who's feared in the world. Pimp admired how Khalil wasn't afraid of anything, quick-tempered and aggressive.

"You thought about what'chu gone do 'bout Deon?" Pimp inquired. Khalil blew smoke from his mouth and nose before responding.

"I ain't sweatin' fool, he ain't no threat," Khalil asserted dryly. Pimp shook his head in disagreement.

"Listen, never take an offensive move without a clear understanding of your opponent. Don't underestimate nobody! You kill the problem at the root. Overstand?" Khalil shook his head yes.

"I hear you, Pimp."

* * *

Traffic was mid when Pimp hopped on I-95 and headed towards Palm Beach. They smoked a few blunts while Pimp laced Khalil up on the play. It took approximately forty-five minutes for them to reach their exit. Pimp made a left on Blue Heron and took it down Avenue J. Once he reached Avenue J, he made a left, passing a sheriff's office. He pulled over by a basketball court, then checked his phone. After sending a text message, he checked Khalil's temperance.

"Wassup, you good?" Pimp asked, lowering the lid of one eye.

"I'm good, big homie. You know how I'm comin'," Khalil retorted, smiling mischievously.

"Say less," Pimp added as his phone alerted. "Shid… Let's do it," Pimp added.

* * *

Afrika entered his one-room apartment with Natalie behind him. Natalie was a mixed breed with a low haircut and a nice shape. Afrika was her drug dealing boyfriend, she'd met him while working at the W Hotel.

"Bae, I'ma make us some drinks. Go find us a movie so we can relax," she insisted.

"I got'chu baby. I want Don Julio," Afrika stated before heading to his room.

"Aahh!" Afrika screamed before dropping to the tile floor. Khalil had cracked him across his head the moment he walked through the door.

"Bae, you okay?" Natalie asked, making her way to the room. When she entered, Pimp pointed his pistol in her face.

"Yeah, bitch! You know what it is! Get'cha ass over there and lay face down," Pimp ordered, motioning with his pistol for her to lay on the floor next to Afrika. She complied.

"Look, man, ain't nothin' in here!" Afrika cried while blood poured from his wound. Pimp stood over Natalie and placed the gun on the back of her head.

"Lie again, I'll blow this bitch shit off, nigga!" Pimp threatened. Afrika hesitated. His lack of haste infuriated Natalie.

"Maan, tell them niggaz where that shit at! You trippin'!" she snapped with a tone of impatience.

"Bitch, shut the fuck up! Ain't shit in here!" Afrika retorted somewhat threateningly.

"Bitch? I got'cha bitch, nigga! Aye, that shit at the bottom of the dresser! Pull them dressers out," Natalie impulsively shouted.

Pimp made haste towards the dresser and pulled out the bottom drawer.

"We lit," Pimp stated as he spotted stacks of money layered at the bottom of the dresser. "Go grab a bag outta the kitchen. Hurry up," Pimp pronounced anxiously.

Khalil made his way to the kitchen and spotted a box of trash bags on the counter. He grabbed the box and some duct tape that sat on top of the microwave, then headed back to the room.

"Here," Khalil said, throwing Pimp the box of trash bags. While Pimp loaded the money in the bag, Khalil decided to tie both victims up.

"Put'cha hands behind ya back," he ordered Afrika.

"Don't kill me, man," Afrika pleaded, putting his hands behind him. Khalil duct taped his hands together, then wrapped tape around his head, eyes, and mouth. Pimp pulled the second dresser out and found ten bricks of molly.

When he looked over to tell Khalil, he noted him slicing Afrika's throat with a scapel that he had gave a fiend two stones for. Khalil grabbed Natalie by her hair and attempted to cut her throat, but Pimp stopped it.

"Not her! She good, lil bra!" Pimp stated. Khalil shot Pimp a dubious look.

"She my ex, she the one lined'em up," Pimp explained.

"Damn, lil nigga, you was just gone cut a bitch throat?" Natalie asked.

"Hell yeah! Shid, you seen our faces," Khalil retorted. Pimp laughed.

"That shit ain't funny! You was suppose to tell him before y'all came in," Natalie stressed, getting up to change her clothes that Khalil had drenched in Afrika's blood.

"That's on me, I apologize," Pimp added.

"Whateva, man. Just drop me to my sister's house wit' my cut and I'm good," Natalie spat before heading to the bathroom.

"You love this bitch?" Khalil whispered. Pimp nodded his head no with a screw face. Moments later, Natalie entered the room and approached Pimp.

"Where my cut?" she asked with her hand extended.

"I'ma give it to you in the car. Come on."

Boc!

Khalil sent one up top, dropping Natalie and spraying Pimp's face and clothes with her blood and brain matter. Pimp wiped his face quickly.

"Damn, lil bra! Let's get the fuck outta here!" Pimp asserted, grabbing a rag to wipe all that they touched. He then grabbed the trash bag full of work and money before they disappeared unnoticed.

* * *

Pimp hopped back on I-95 and headed back to "The City of No Pity" a little richer than before.

"We hit good," Pimp stated, elated.

"Hell yeah," Khalil agreed, dapping Pimp up.

"Why you hit the hoe though?" Pimp inquired.

"Shid, she seen our faces! Plus, you say you ain't love the hoe. That was a no brainer," Khalil retorted. Pimp gazed at him, then smiled.

"I respect it. Peep this though. I ain't callin' you Khalil no more. You way too treacherous for that. From now on, I'm addressin' you as Killa!" Khalil smirked while nodding his head in approval.

Chapter 10
(I See Dead People)

Khalil was laid back in his room smoking a blunt, thinking about Marcia, when he noticed a figure in his peripheral. Out of pure instinct he clutched his pistol.

"Da fuck?" he mumbled, squinting to get a better view of the shadowy figure.

"Who da fuck is that?" Khalil asked, sitting up in his bed, facing the door.

"Oh, nah you don't know me, huh?" The shadowy figure responded as her identity became apparent. "Maan… why did you kill me?" Natalie asked with a bloody hole in her head.

"Fuck!" Khalil yelled, squeezing off multiple shots. Boc! Boc! Boc!

Khalil jumped out of his sleep, sweating and clutching his Glock. He did a quick survey of the room, then jumped up to cut the light on. Khalil's heart was beating rapidly as the episode of killing Natalie kept replaying in his mind. His door opened and his mother stepped in.

"Boy, what'chu in here screaming for?" Penny questioned, spotting the pistol in his hand.

"Nothin', I'm good! Can you please get out of my room?" Khalil replied, irritated.

"Nigga, this my fuckin' house! I ain't gotta do shit! And, what the fuck you doin' wit' a gun in my house?" she spat, seething. "You gone have to get that shit out my house or get the fuck out!"

"Maan, all the money I be givin' you! I ain't goin' nowhere, you trippin! You see where we live, I'm keepin' my shit!" Khalil snapped. Penny continued to rant. In the middle of her ranting, Khalil reached in his pocket and threw a wad of hundreds in her direction. Penny's words were cut short as she bent down to pick up all the money.

"Nah, can you please get out? Please!" he asked.

"You lil motherfucka! You gone end up just like ya daddy!" Penny asserted before leaving and slamming the door. Khalil quickly rolled himself a blunt and sparked it. He then checked his phone for the time. It was 2:42 in the morning. Moments later, there was a knock at the door, then Kaleb entered. Khalil had a unit on his face but quickly relaxed the muscles in his face when he noted that Kaleb had his hands up.

"Look bra, don't trip on me. I just came in here to check on you," Kaleb stated sincerely. Khalil inhaled then exhaled deeply.

"You straight. I'm aight though, just had a fucked-up dream," Khalil replied, taking another pull from his blunt.

"What the dream about?" Kaleb asked. Khalil blew smoke in Kaleb's face before answering.

"I see dead people," Khalil admitted in a jokingly manner mimicking Haley Joel Osment from the movie *The Sixth Sense*. Kaleb fanned the reefer smoke away from his face.

"You wit' the bullshit early this mornin'." Khalil chuckled sinisterly.

"Moma say you gotta gun," Kaleb implied. Khalil slid his hand under his pillow, grabbed his pistol and handed it to Kaleb. Kaleb grabbed it, holding it awkwardly. He examined it in disbelief, then looked in his brother's eyes.

"You trippin'!" Kaleb pronounced, using his shirt to wipe his prints off the gun, before handing it back to Khalil. Khalil just blew smoke in Kaleb's direction.

"What type of shit Pimp got'chu on?" Kaleb asked, making his way towards the door. Khalil chuckled again before replying.

"Some shit you can't stomach. So, do me a favor and go that way! Make sho' you close the door behind you, Moma's boy."

Kaleb shook his head in pity, then made his way out of the room. As soon as Khalil got up to turn off the light, his phone rang. It read "Erica." Khalil sat ambivalently as the phone continued to ring. He was still upset that Erica had told Pimp that he had answered the phone. Khalil exhaled deeply, then answered.

"Yeah?" he answered with a sniffle of disdain.

"So, that's how you answer the phone?" asked Erica, unfazed by Khalil's apparent temperament.

"Hell yeah, shid…! Why the fuck you told Pimp that we talked on the phone?" he snapped.

"First off, relax. Calm down, it's not that serious. I told him that I called his phone, looking for him, but you answered. How was I supposed to know that you had his phone?" Erica fabricated.

This lyin' ass bitch! Khalil thought. Pimp had already told him that he' told Erica to call him to see if he'd pick up. He decided to play along.

"Well, Pimp ain't here," Khalil assured.

"Damn! I drove way down here to Fort Pierce for blow, and Pimp can't even be located," she cried. Khalil's mind began to race.

"Shid, what'chu lookin' for?"

"I wanted six more zips."

"Look, I got one left. If you want it, it's gone be two bandz."

"That's no problem. Let me get it."

"Meet me at the Bails bondsmen on 25th Street in the back parking lot," Khalil enunciated.

"It ain't no bullshit, is it?" she pried.

"Don't play me like that, I got'cha," he assured.

"Okay, I'll be there in ten minutes," she retorted. Click!

Khalil quickly took 3.5 out of the ounce of coke and replaced it with 3.5 of no taste no smell cut. He then tucked his pistol and headed down the street to the Bail Bondsmen.

* * *

Khalil mobbed down Avenue I with his hands tucked in his Alexander McQueen skull-print cotton hoodie. His thoughts were on the dream he'd just had, when a car cut in front of him on the corner of 24th and Avenue I. Khalil, already clutching his pistol, semi-snatched it out, but quickly tucked it once he saw that it was a cop.

"What'chu doin' out here, boy!" The Klansman in a cop uniform sneered.

"Mindin' my own, like you should be, kracka!" Khalil retorted venomously.

"Get'cha hands outta your pocket," the cop demanded, opening his door. Khalil backed up, snatched out and blew his pistol.

Boc! Boc! Boc! Boc! Boc!

Before the cop could step out of his vehicle, red tipped hollows peppered his face, neck, and chest, leaving him slumped under the moon. Khalil ran across the street behind the deserted substation and ran through the park. When Khalil made it through the field, he cut through the fence and walked slowly down 24th Street. Moments later, his phone rang.

"Yeah?" he answered, slightly out of breath.

"Umm, I'ma have to meet'chu somewhere else, because it's a police car parked on the corner behind the Bails Bondsmen. It look like something wrong with him, like he dead or something," Erica exclaimed.

"Yeah, I seen that. I'm on 24th behind the ELKS, hurry up and come get me," he responded calmly.

"Okay, I'm on my way."

"Aight." Click! Khalil was calm, but his thoughts were running rapidly. He couldn't believe he'd just killed a cop.

Having dope and a gun on him, he knew that was a one-way ticket to the Bing. So, his decision to kill first was valid. A Hellcat Durango turned the corner, prompting Khalil to clutch his heat. When the headlights began to blink, he knew it was Erica. She slowed down beside him and he jumped in.

"Wassup baby, you okay?" Erica questioned.

"Yeah, everythang G's," he replied. Erica began sniffing the air.

"Why you smell like smoke?"

"Shid, I just smoked a Black & Mild," he lied. Having an outside gun range, Erica knew the smell of gun smoke well. She decided not to speak on it.

"Oh, okay. You got the blow?" she asked.

"Yeah, I got it," Khalil assured, handing her the zip. Erica handed him the money, then stopped the truck to take a bump of coke.

"Ummm!" she moaned. "This shit good," Erica admitted.

"I know it. Peep though, get in the wind," Khalil asserted, hounding the rearview mirror expecting cops to surround the truck at any moment.

"No problem, where you goin'?" she asked, pulling off.

"Shid, if you don't mind, I wanna go back to the reservation with you for a few days." Erica glanced at Khalil knowingly. She knew something was wrong and decided to help him out.

"If that's what you want, I don't mind. You wanna go grab something before we head out?"

"Nawl, I'm good," Khalil said, pulling his phone out to make a call. The caller answered on the fourth ring.

"Yeah, who is this?" Kaleb answered groggily.

"This Khalil. Wake ya ass up, nigga."

"I'm up! Wassup, man?" Kaleb whined, wiping the cold from his eye.

"Listen! I got some shit in my room, don't let nobody in my shit!"

"Aight. Where you at?"

"I'ma be gone for a few days. Just watch my shit, man," Khalil advised semi-threateningly. Click! Khalil hung the phone up and could hear sirens in the distance.

"You good?" Erica asked.

"Yeah, I'm aight."

Chapter 11

(Bitch!)

Kaleb got dressed for school, then went into Khalil's room out of curiosity. He headed straight to the closet and opened it. Designer clothes and shoes littered the closet from top to bottom.

"Damn," Kaleb mumbled as he began to search through shoe boxes. After coming up with nothing, he closed the closet door then stood by the bed. An ashtray on the nightstand was filled with blunt roaches, and Khalil's bed was in disarray.

"What the fuck he want me to watch?" Kaleb muttered, lifting the front of the mattress. There was nothing beneath it. Kaleb glanced around the room, then back at the mattress. He lifted the back of it and spotted what needed to be watched. It was a hole in the box spring. When Kaleb looked in the hole, he spotted layers of money and what appeared to be two bricks of dope. He quickly sat the mattress back in position and got up to leave when the door opened.

"Kaleb? Where Khalil at?" Penny asked, clearly high on molly.

"I don't know, Ma," he answered making his way out of the room.

"Well, what'chu doin' in his room?"

"I was checkin' to see if I left my phone in his room. It was on the nightstand," Kaleb lied, showing her the phone as he headed downstairs.

"Oh, okay. Have a good day in school, baby," Penny asserted, closing Khalil's door behind her.

"Yes, ma'am!" Kaleb yelled before leaving out of the door. On his way to the bus stop, Kaleb pulled out his phone and called Khalil. After the first ring, he was sent to voicemail. He tried several more times but received the same results.

"Damn, this nigga ain't picking up," Kaleb mumbled to himself.

"Wassup, nephew? You workin'?" a fiend pried fidgety in her manner.

"What the hell you talkin' 'bout?" Kaleb asked, not knowing that the fiend was mistaking him for Khalil.

"Where the dope at, nephew?"

"Maan, look here, I'on sell that shit!" Kaleb snapped, trying to keep it pushing and make it to the bus stop.

"Come on, nephew. I'll suck yo' dick. Let auntie eat that dick up," she suggested, trying to close the space between them.

"Aye man, get the fuck away from me!" Kaleb snapped, moving towards her aggressively.

"That's alright, nephew!" she yelled right before Kaleb made it to his bus stop.

"You got me fucked up!" he retorted, but it was too late. Everyone at the bus stop erupted in laughter.

“Damn, Kaleb, you that desperate?” Janay clowned. “I gotta cousin for you, if it’s that bad,” she continued.

“Maan…fuck you Janay,” he retorted, waving his hand at her in a dismissive manner.

“Nawl, fuck wit me! And, where my husband at?” Janay replied, referring to Khalil.

“Fuck you!” Kaleb snapped. Janay laughed it off. Moments later a horn blew, startling Kaleb.

“Kaleb, pull up on me!” Pimp yelled out. Kaleb approached Pimp’s vehicle.

“Wassup, Pimp?”

“Wassup wit’ it, lil homie? You aight?”

“Yeah, I’m good. Wassup though?”

“I been tryin’ to reach Khalil, but he ain’t pickin’ up. You seen’em?” Pimp asked, sparking a blunt.

“He called me last night and told me that he was gone be out of bounds for a few days. He ain’t tell me where he was at or where he goin’,” Kaleb informed. Pimp shook his head up and down while rubbing his chin.

“Fasho, lil homie. You good?” Pimp asked, peeling off two crispy blue-face hunnids and handing them to Kaleb.

“Appreciate’chu, Pimp. I gotta game comin’ up. You think you can pull up?”

“Just let me know where and when. I’ll be there, lil homie,” Pimp promised.

“Bet that up, Pimp,” Kaleb responded, dapping Pimp up and watching him pull off.

Chapter 12

(Shut the Fuck up!)

Gerby pulled into one of his houses on Mayflower Street in a dark blue 2023 Genesis G90, with his brother Fernando behind him in a white 2320 Genesis GV60. Gerby hopped out and headed to Fernando's vehicle and leaned into the window.

"Aight, bra. I'm finna do a lil inventory then take it on in to wifey," Gerby pronounced, dapping his little brother up.

"You sho' you don't want me to help you?" Fernando replied.

"Nawl, I got Kia in there. I'ma prolly knock her down, so I'on need ju all in ma video," Gerby remarked, tapping on the roof of Fernando's whip before walking off.

"Aight family, love!" Fernando retorted, pulling out of the driveway.

"Love!" Gerby replied, walking under the carport and sticking his key in a side door that led to the kitchen. When he entered the home, the stench of griot and pikliz polluted the air.

"Damn, it smell good in here! Kia! Kia, baby, where you at?"

Gerby noted the Haitian food on the stove. He grabbed some griot, threw it in his mouth then headed to Kia's room chewing slovenly. Kia was Gerby's side piece whom he had a baby boy with, unbeknownst to his wife.

"Kia, baby!" Gerby called out as he entered her room. When he spotted Kia, his eyes bulged in confusion.

"Kia!" he yelled. Moments later when he realized what was taking place, he pulled his Glock 19.

"Pussy nigga, don't move!" Pimp snapped, placing the tip of his 911 on the back of Gerby's head.

"Fuck," Gerby ululated, disappointed that he'd been caught slipping. Pimp seemed to have materialized out of nowhere and got the drop on him. Kia was in clear view in front of him, tied to a chair with duct tape on her mouth.

"Yeah, you know the vibe. Drop it or get dropped, nigga," Pimp demanded, putting pressure on the back of Gerby's head. Gerby dropped his pistol.

"Look bra, I ain't…" SMACK! Pimp slapped Gerby in the back of his head, dropping him vehemently. Kia's cries were muffled while Pimp quickly bent down to pick the pistol up. Gerby's hands were trying to massage away the pain through his dreads while Kia went into pure panic mode, hyperventilating.

"You know the vibe. Get the fuck up and show me where that work at," Pimp ordered.

"Assssha… fffuck! Maan, ain't shit in here," Gerby claimed, now on his knees, still clutching his head.

"Oh yeah?" Pimp asked, walking over to the baby's crib and pointing his gun inside. "Look here!" Pimp stated. Gerby looked up and saw Pimp standing over his baby boy.

"Bra, wait! Listen, ain't shit—" Boc! Boc! Pimp let off two shots next to the baby's head. The gun was so loud that the baby's ears began to bleed. Kia went into full hysteria, crying and shaking uncontrollably.

"Aight, my nigga! It's in the refrigerator! The dope in the refrigerator, man. Fuck!" Gerby cried. Seconds later, the baby began to cry. Kia and Gerby silently thanked the creator.

"Get up, nigga, take me to it! Hurry the fuck up," Pimp snapped, pointing his gun at Gerby.

"Aight, you got it, fam, don't shoot. This shit ain't nothin, you can get it," Gerby claimed, standing to his feet and heading to the kitchen.

"If this shit ain't nothin', then why the fuck you lied about it being in here?" Pimp stated through clenched teeth, smacking Gerby in the back of his head again. He stumbled but didn't fall.

"Tighten up, nigga!" Pimp declared once Gerby reached the refrigerator.

"Don't shoot me, bra," Gerby pleaded, opening the door to the refrigerator.

"Shut the fuck up and man up!" Gerby took all the food from the side of the door and placed it in the refrigerator. He then began to rip the panel off the refrigerator door. When he finally tore it off, ten bricks of heroin fell to the floor.

"Aight nigga, where the money at?" Pimp asked his adrenaline pumping profusely.

"It's in the backseat of my car in a knapsack," Gerby said with his hands semi raised. Boc! Boc! Boc!

Pimp put three hot ones in Gerby's chest, dropping him.

"Stupid nigga!" Pimp spat, grabbing a Winn-Dixie bag out of the fridge to put the bricks in. He sat the bag on the counter, then headed to Kia's room.

"Wassup, ma, you good?" Pimp asked. A crying Kia shook her head up and down.

"Right," Pimp asserted, turning to leave. Moments later, he reappeared and fired four shots at Kia, hitting her in the neck and face. Pimp grabbed the bag off the counter, headed to Gerby's car to grab the knapsack, then disappeared into the night.

Chapter 13

(Sweet thang)

It was 8:15 pm when Khalil slipped inside his mother's apartment. The living room was deserted, but he could hear Kaleb's voice coming from upstairs. Khalil headed upstairs to his room and went straight to his stash spot. One of his stacks of money had been tampered with, and a brick of molly had been opened. Khalil was instantly inflamed and headed to Kaleb's room. When he kicked Kaleb's door open, he was laid back in his bed on the phone.

"Bitch ass nigga, get-cha ass off the phone!" Khalil barked viciously. Kaleb balled up his face in confusion.

"Aye, let me call you back. Yeah!" Kaleb hung the phone up and rose from his bed. "Wassup?" Kaleb asked. Khalil snatched his pistol out and pointed it in his brother's face.

"Where the fuck my money and dope at, nigga?" Khalil snapped through clenched teeth.

"Bra, I ain't touch yo' shit! On everything I love!"

"Yes, the fuck you did, bitch ass nigga! I dun killed for less, nigga, I should pop yo' shit!" Khalil threatened.

"Killed for less? You know what? I told ju I ain't touch yo' shit! Fuck it, put the gun down, killa! Put that shit down and face me like a man! You suppose to be my mothafuckin' brother, and you gotta gun pointed in my face!" Kaleb expressed, tears falling from his eyes. "Put it down, I'll beat the fuck out'chu," Kaleb swore. Khalil bit his bottom lip and shook his head up and down. He then placed the gun on Kaleb's dresser.

"Tighten up, sweet thang," Khalil taunted. Kaleb rushed Khalil like a mad man throwing two wild punches. Khalil weaved Kaleb's right but got caught by his left.

"Oooh, okay, sweet thang!" Khalil taunted, throwing up the blocking mechanism known as the Peek-A-Boo created by Joe Frazier. Khalil blocked three of Kaleb's punches then pushed forward, causing Kaleb to fall on the bed.

"Mmm-hmm!" Khalil pronounced, rushing forward and stomping Kaleb in his face with his right foot. He followed up with a straight two-piece combination straight down the pipe.

"Aahh!" Kaleb yelled, covering his face. Khalil grabbed Kaleb by his legs then pulled him off the bed, causing him to hit his head on the floor.

"Umm-umm! Don't holla nah, Moma's boy," Khalil clowned, bending over to pepper Kaleb with combinations. Kaleb was kicking and scratching for his life when Penny opened the door.

"What the fuck is you doin'?" she yelled, rushing in the room. "Get the fuck off him!" Penny screamed, grabbing and pulling Khalil by his shirt. Out of pure instinct, Khalil swiveled and slapped the shit out of his mother, sending her crashing to the floor.

"Oooww, you lil mothafucka!" she screamed holding her face.

"Bitch!" Khalil snapped, grabbing his pistol off the dresser. He rushed forward and commenced to pistol whipping his mother. "Bitch! I know you went in my shit, hoe!" Khalil snapped while continuing his onslaught. Kaleb managed to get to his feet and rushed Khalil, causing him to crash against the front door. Khalil pushed off the door and spun around, throwing Kaleb off of him. Khalil pointed his pistol in Kaleb's face.

"You wanna die nigga! Huh?" Khalil asked through clenched teeth. "It's yo' fuckin fault! I told ju to watch my shit, nigga!"

"Come on, bra! You trippin'! That's Moma!" Kaleb cried.

"Nigga, what?" Khalil retorted, placing the barrel on his brother's nose.

"Khalil, don't!" Penny yelled. Khalil pushed Kaleb in his face with the gun, then turned towards his mother. He went in his pocket and threw two thousand dollars in her face.

"You ever fuck wit' my shit again… I'ma kill you!"

* * *

Khalil headed to his room while Kaleb tended to his mother's wounds. Once in the room, he closed the door, locked it behind him and sat on his bed, placing his pistol next to him. He sparked a blunt, inhaled deeply and exhaled slowly. Tears began to cascade down his face as he fell into a reminiscent state about his childhood abuse. He flashed back to a traumatic experience when he was five years old.

"Khalil! Khalil, wake yo' ass up!" Penny screamed. Khalil opened his eyes slowly and began to wipe the cold from them.

"Yes, ma'am?" he retorted tiredly.

"Boy! I know mothafuckin' well you didn't piss in that mothafuckin' bed!" she yelled, snatching the sheets off of a pissy Khalil.

"No, ma'am," Khalil replied, terrified of the consequences for pissing the bed.

"You a black ass lie! Aye, Cecil! Cecil, come here!" Penny yelled, calling out to her boyfriend at the time. Within

seconds, Cecil barged into the room, reeking of liquor and cigarettes.

"What the hell he dun did, nah?" Cecil asked.

"His ass dun pissed up my damn sheets," Penny instigated.

"Oh, yeah?" Cecil asked, removing his belt.

"Noooo!" yelled Khalil, who began to quiver in tears. Khalil spotted Kaleb standing in the doorway with terror in his eyes.

"Kaleb! Tell'em it wasn't me! Please! Tell'em you the one who peed!" Khalil cried frantically. Instead of saving his brother from being abused, Kaleb turned away and ran.

"Stop lyin' on my baby! Kaleb don't pee in the bed!" Penny exclaimed.

"Come here, boy." Cecil demanded, handing the belt to Penny before rushing Khalil and putting him in the DDT position. Instead of DDT'ing Khalil, Cecil sat on the edge of the bed and locked his legs around the back of Khalil's.

"Beat that ass, Penny," he taunted.

"No, Moma please," Khalil cried. Smack! Smack! Smack!

Penny showed no empathy for Khalil's pleas. She beat Khalil's back and ass as if he were a long-time opposition. When Cecil felt like it was enough, he released a battered and distraught Khalil.

"Back up, Penny!" he ordered. She did as she was told.

"Nah, since you like pissin' in the bed, lil nigga, suck on them sheets!" Cecil told Khalil. Khalil began to cry harder.

"It wasn't even me! It was Kaleb!" he cried.

"Come on, nah. You goin' too far, bae," Penny asserted.

"Shut the fuck up before I beat'cho ass!" Cecil threatened.

Penny backed away with her hands up. Even though Penny was abusive to Khalil, he still loved her. He quickly began to suck the sheets, afraid that if he didn't, Cecil would beat his mother.

"Yeah, lil nigga! Before you ever think of pissin' the bed again, think of the taste of that piss." Cecil laughed before forcing Penny out of the room and leaving behind her.

***

Khalil snapped out of the flashback and instantly wanted to go back into Kaleb's room and kill them both. He never understood why Kaleb didn't own up to his peeing in the bed, and why would his mother let a man who wasn't his father abuse him. Despite all this, he loved them both. The downside was that a life fraught with hardship and abuse had turned him into a killa… a treacherous youngin'.

Chapter 14

(You Ain't Sayin' Shit)

The next morning when Khalil awoke, his suspension from school was up. He sat up in his bed and began to wipe the cold from his eyes. After replaying the events from last night in his mind, Khalil got up and hopped in the shower. Fifteen minutes later, he hopped out and got dressed for school. He removed all his schoolbooks from his bookbag and loaded all his money and dope into it. After rolling a blunt, he tucked his pistol and headed towards his door, when there was a knock. Seconds later, Pimp walked in.

"Top of the mornin', Killa," Pimp greeted, dapping Khalil up.

"Wass good, big homie?" Khalil retorted.

"Back to school, huh?"

"Yeah, I gotta get the hell away from here, before I fuck around and do somethin' to deez people, man," Khalil asserted. Pimp shook his head in understanding.

"Yeah, ya Moma told me what happened. You went a lil too hard, but nah you see why I don't let her come to my house." Khalil nodded his head. "Here," Pimp said reaching in his pocket, grabbing a Cuban and putting it around Khalil's neck. He then pulled out a rollie and placed it on his wrist. Khalil smiled with appreciation. "Come on," Pimp pronounced, heading out of the room and down the stairs with Khalil behind him. Pimp opened the door and stepped outside. When Khalil stepped outside he saw a smoke gray truck parked next to Pimp's scat.

"Damn! That bitch clean! What that is?" Khalil asked.

"Oh, that? That's a 2021 Aston Martin," Pimp informed, smiling.

"One of my white power plays, owed me some money. I gave him a few ounces and we called it even. You like it?"

"Hell yeah!"

"Good, kuz it's yours!" Pimp stated, throwing Khalil the keys. Khalil caught the keys.

"Real shit?" he asked excitedly.

"I ever played games wit'chu? Come on, man, you my lil partna! Get in!" Khalil hopped in the driver's seat while Pimp hopped in the passenger's. Moments later, Kaleb stepped outside and spotted Khalil in the driver's seat He gazed at Khalil for a moment, then headed to the bus stop.

"Listen to me. That's ya brother and he love you, man. I know ya Moma treat him different from you, but it ain't his fault. You hear me?" Khalil shook his head yes but wasn't really feeling it.

"Yo moma was wrong for goin' in yo shit, but she still yo' moma. You only get one of them and mines gone. Nah, I ain't tryna be yo' daddy or nothin', I just fuck wit'chu," Pimp expressed.

"I fuck wit'chu too, Pimp," Khalil added.

"When you get outta school, call me asap! you hear me?" Khalil nodded his head yes.

"Okay, nah, where you was when I called looking for you?" Pimp questioned. Khalil glanced at Pimp, then back through the windshield.

"I had to lay low for a few days. I was at Marcia's house," he lied, not wanting Pimp to know that he was with Erica.

“Lay low, for what?” Pimp pried. Khalil paused for a moment before replying.

“The other mornin’, I gotta call for a play. I get dressed to come out and meet my play, when a police swerve in front of me at the corner. I got dope and a pistol on me, so when he tried to hop out on me, I blew my shit. Man down, I had to get low, fam,” Khalil explained. Pimp chuckled.

“I had a feelin’ that was you. Shid, they ain’t gotta suspect or nothin’, you should be good. Don’t repeat this to nobody else. You hear me?”

“I hear you…”

“Right, call me as soon as you get outta school,” Pimp enunciated, dapping Khalil up before stepping out of his truck. He stood in the driveway and watched Khalil pull off. Pimp didn’t have any kids, which is why he took to Khalil. His mother used to treat him different from his brother and sister too, so he felt Khalil’s pain. He knew that he had created an animal-type beast, but after seeing what Khalil had done to his own mother and brother… He knew Khalil was way beyond that… He was a treacherous youngin’!

* * *

Kaleb was on his way to the bus stop replaying the events from last night in his mind. Kaleb had a bust lip and a black eye which he could live with. However, seeing his brother pistol whip his mother was something entirely different. He didn’t recognize his twin anymore and worried that he might have to do something to him. While deep in thought, Khalil pulled alongside Kaleb and rolled his passenger window down.

“What up, twin? You wanna ride to school?” Khalil offered.

“I’on want shit from you, nigga,” Kaleb retorted as he continued walking to the bus stop with Khalil beside him.

"Come on, nah! Brothers fight all the time," Khalil added. Kaleb stopped abruptly, then walked closer to Khalil's truck.

"Nigga, you pistol whipped Moma! Fuck is you talkin' 'bout, man?"

"Okay, I admit. Shit got a lil outta hand. I understand yo' frustration, but if you woulda kept an eye on my shit, this woulda never happened," Khalil explained calmly. Kaleb bared an expression of disbelief as anger began to spread through his bones pulsing.

"Nigga, fuck you!" Kaleb spat.

"Aight, bra, when you wanna talk about it, I'ma be around," Khalil asserted, pulling off and stopping at the bus stop.

"Fuck is wrong wit' this nigga?" Kaleb muttered to himself.

* * *

"Wassup, Janay? You wanna ride wit' me to school?" Khalil asked.

"Hell, yeah!" Janay replied, hopping into the passenger's seat. Khalil pulled off, glancing in the mirror at his brother.

"So, who truck you stole?" Janay asked, looking around. Khalil chuckled.

"This my shit, you trippin'!" he pronounced, sparking a blunt.

"Umm-huh! I know you ain't got no license, and you prolly got dope and a gun in here."

"If you feel like that, then why you hopped in my shit?"

"Come on, nah!" Janay said, rubbing her hand inside Khalil's inner thigh. "You know I like that gangsta shit," she added, grabbing a hand full of dick.

"And you know I like to get my dick licked. So, stop all that talkin', and eat a nigga up," Khalil advised.

"You ain't sayin' shit," Janay retorted, slipping Khalil's dick from his designers and chewing him all the way to school.

Chapter 15

(Wassup Nah?)

When Khalil pulled into the teaching staff's parking lot, Janay was still eating him up. He had saliva all over his Sol jeans and had to practically pull Janay by her hair to remove her mouth from his dick.

"Maan, look what you did to my fuckin' pants!" Khalil snapped. Janay wiped her mouth and smiled shamelessly.

"If it ain't sloppy, it ain't real toppy," Janay proudly stated.

"Tsss…! Maan, hand me them sweats out the backseat," Khalil demanded as he began to remove his Levi's. Janay grabbed the Fendi sweats and handed them to Khalil.

"So, when you gone let me sit on that dick?" Janay questioned.

"Be patient, good dick comes to those who wait," he clowned pulling the sweats up and transferring the money from the Sol's to the Fendi's.

"I guess," Janay retorted. "Let me get some money for lunch." Khalil peeled off a blue face hunnid and handed it to her.

"Thank you. I'm ridin' home wit'chu after school?"

"I'on know yet. I'ma let'chu know, though," Khalil asserted, stepping out of his truck. Janay got out behind him.

"You know you can't park here, right?" she mentioned.

"Fuck the krackaz!" he retorted, heading to campus with Janay in tow. As soon as Khalil got close to the cafeteria, he could hear his name being called. When Khalil turned around, he saw Marcia traversing across the courtyard, making her way towards him.

"Janay, I'ma fuck wit'chu later," Khalil proclaimed.

"Okay, you know the number. Call me, whenever," Janay replied, smiling before walking off.

"Khalil," Marcia called out with her arms outstretched. Khalil grabbed her and pulled her in close, hugging her tightly.

"Wassup wit it?" he retorted.

"I missed you, why you haven't been callin' or coming to see me?" Marcia cried, unwrapping her arms from around Khalil. "Was it because of my brother?" she added stepping back to examine Khalil's new drip.

"Nawl, I missed you too. I been meaning to get at'chu, I just been on go lately."

"I see that! Khalil, what'chu doin?" Marcia asked with her hands on her thick curvy hips.

"Shid, I'm tryna go to class and get my education, but'chu gotta nigga under interrogation and shit," Khalil retorted.

"Don't do that. You know I mean well," she explained.

"Yeah, I know. You goin' to breakfast?" he questioned.

"Wassup, Khalil?" a familiar voice asked. Khalil turned and noticed Deon standing behind him.

"Nigga, you know what it is! What'chu wanna do?" Khalil snapped, attempting to walk towards Deon.

"Khalil, no!" Marica pleaded, placing her hand on his chest.

"I'on want no smoke wit'cha, homie. I just pulled up to tell you, that shit dead," Deon asserted, smiling.

"The fuck you smiling for?" Khalil barked.

"I see you sauced up, drippin' and shit! Boy, you done came a long way! Put a nigga on!" Deon clowned.

"Get the fuck out my face before you die on these kracka'z campus, stupid nigga!" Khalil threatened with blood in his eyes. Marcia's brow creased with astonishment.

"Khalil, let's just walk away, please," she begged. Khalil looked at Marcia's titillating light brown eyes, then back at Deon.

"I'ma catch you later, killa!" Deon declared, winking at Khalil before walking away.

"Facts, bitch ass nigga!" Khalil retorted.

"You aight?" Kaleb asked, approaching from the side. Khalil turned to face his brother.

"I'm always aight, nigga," Khalil affirmed, putting his arm around Marcia and walking off. Kaleb shook his head then headed to class.

* * *

When the last bell of the day rang, all students rushed the halls, headed towards their buses. Khalil had been texting back and forth with Marica and Janay between classes and decided that he would let Marcia ride home with him. She confirmed that she would meet him in the bus loading zone after school. As Khalil made his way through the hallway, a crowd slowly began to form around him.

"Yeah killa, wassup nah? All that talk about killin' me on these kracka'z campus and shit, what nah?" Deon instigated with a devilish grin on his face. Khalil chuckled before responding.

"Fuck you went and got these niggas for? To die in front of 'em? Aight, you wanna die, brang yo' dumb ass back here," Khalil pronounced slowly backing his way into a cut out of sight. As soon as Khalil slid his hand into his backpack, Janay appeared out of nowhere and hit one of

Deon's homies in the face with a two-piece combination, causing him to stumble.

"Pussy niggaz, get back!" she declared, throwing her set up.

"Hoe, you trippin'!" Poodle proclaimed, holding his jawbone.

"Wassup wit'chu niggaz?" Kaleb asked, dropping his backpack and pulling up his Chrome heart pants.

"Hey! Hey, what the hell going on over here?" Mr. Heart yelled, walking in between the crowd. Mr. Heart was a dean at the school. Khalil removed his hand from inside his backpack and slipped it back on.

"Nothin', we just goofin' off, Mr. Heart," Deon retorted.

"Y'all get the hell outta here and get on your buses… now!" Mr. Heart demanded.

"Yes, sir," Deon retorted, nodding his head to his homies, signaling them to retreat.

"Khalil, you just got back! You're treading on thin ice," Mr. Heart threatened.

"Yeah, whateva man," Khalil remarked, blowing past him. Mr. Heart shook his head before walking away.

"Bra, you aight?" Kaleb asked, walking behind Khalil.

"Yeah, I'm good." Khalil noted Janay walking beside him and put his arm around her.

"You a solid one. Good looking out, kuz I was finna smoke one of them goofy ass niggaz," Khalil admitted, kissing Janay on the cheek.

"I knew you had a gun," Janay proclaimed, smiling.

"Shhhh!" Khalil responded, making her smile.

"Look, bra, I'm finna hop on the bus," Kaleb stated, reaching his fist out for Khalil to bump. Khalil eyed it for a moment, then bumped fists with his brother.

"Aight, good lookin' out," Khalil asserted.

"Fasho," Kaleb responded before walking ahead of them.

"Janay, you ridin' wit' me," Khalil asserted.

"Okay."

"Marcia ridin' wit' us though," he added.

Janay shrugged her shoulders.

"I'on care. As long as I'm wit'chu, I'm there," Janay assured. Khalil laughed, then kissed Janay on her cheek again. When they made it to the bus loading zone, Marcia was waiting for him. She was all smiles until Khalil approached, with Janay beside him.

"Wassup, Marcia," Khalil greeted, hugging her.

"Wassup?" she retorted, unwrapping her arms from around Khalil while gazing at Janay quizzically.

"Hey, Marcia," Janay spoke, smiling knowingly.

"Hey," Marica responded dryly.

"Janay ridin' wit' us," he confirmed. Marcia's expression was that of confusion.

"Khalil, we haven't spoken or seen each other in days. I was hoping to spend some time alone wit'chu," she whined.

"I know, I'ma just take her home, then we can vibe." Marcia sucked her teeth before inhaling and exhaling deeply in frustration.

"Janay, nothing against you, but I'm straight. Just call me whenever you get a chance," Marcia asserted before walking off to catch her bus.

"Bye, Marcia!" Janay sang in a taunting manner. Marcia threw her hand up and kept it pushing.

"You ain't right," Khalil stated, smiling.

"What?" Janay retorted, matching his smile.

Chapter 16
(You My Nigga)

Khalil had been getting his dick sucked the whole drive from school, while on the phone with Marcia. He finally got her to hang up when he pulled his truck on Taylor's creek ditch bank. Pop! Janay sucked the head of Khalil's dick before popping it out of her mouth to speak.

"Damn! 'Bout time that hoe hung up! The fuck? Hoe, it ain't shit you can do to keep me from wettin' that dick up! She know what time it is," Janay stated, pulling her soaked panties from under her Dior skirt. Khalil chuckled.

"Wet that dick up, huh?" he asked.

"You know what it is, too," she retorted climbing on top of Khalil. She grabbed his shaft, guided it to her opening and wiggled down on all of him.

"Shhhit…!" They moaned in unison as the warmth from their flesh collided. Khalil grabbed both of Janay's soft, bite-size cheeks as she rose to the tip of his dick, and dropped rapidly, then instantly switched into a slow grind.

"Ssss… ooowW, this dick good," she admitted, leaning forward to suck on Khalil's neck and ears. Khalil grabbed Janay by her hair, yanking her mouth away from his neck. He then placed both of his hands around her neck and began to thrust upward in an erratic rhythm.

"Aahhhaaah!" Janay cried, her moan semi-suppressed due to being mildly suffocated. Janay had always fantasized about asphyxiation, and now she was experiencing it firsthand.

"Umm-hhmm!" Khalil boasted, biting on his bottom lip while lunging deeper into her womb.

"Fuck! This pussy wet!" he added as the sound of Janay's pussy juices began to mimic stirred mac-n-cheese. When Khalil felt her pussy muscles constricting around his dick, he applied more pressure around her neck and gave her all he had, until a copious flow squirted and sprayed all over Khalil's dick, pants, and apple butter upholstery.

"Da fuck?" Khalil yelled, letting go of her neck. Janay inhaled loudly, chasing her breath, all while leaning forward to grab the headrest and bounce on Khalil's dick wildly.

"Hhhaaaaaaha… my fuckin' God! Ssss… ooooww, shit this a good ass nut!" she cried while still squirting and shaking repeatedly.

"Fuck!" Khalil asserted, cummin' behind her.

"Sss, ooow, yeah! Nut in this pussy, daddy!" she added, biting her bottom lip and slowly grinding on his dick until both of their orgasms subsided. Khalil lifted Janay from his lap and tossed her into the passenger seat.

"Really?" she exclaimed.

"Shut the fuck up! You done fucked up another pair of my pants and shit! You lucky that pussy was good," he remarked. Janay smiled.

"Yeah, nigga, real wap! I need somethin' to clean up wit'."

"Here," Khalil retorted, pulling off his shirt and handing it to Janay to wipe with.

"Damn, I know this pussy good, nah. You done gave me the shirt off yo' back to clean it," she clowned.

"Whateva, nigga," he shot back, grabbing her panties and handing them to her.

"Umum! You keep'em. You earned them, good dick."

"Man, here! Fuck I'ma do wit'em?" Khalil retorted, lighting a blunt and stepping out of the truck. Janay slid her panties inside the side of the passenger door, then stepped out too.

"I gotta let my shit air out! You done sprayed pussy juice all over my shit!" he declared, walking closer to the bank to look at the murky water. Janay walked up and hugged him from behind.

"Shut up," she said in a child-like manner. Khalil took a pull from his blunt, then exhaled in deep thought. "What'chu thinkin' 'bout?" Janay asked. Khalil chuckled.

"I'm thinkin' how you saved me from killin' one of them niggaz in school today. You ran up, poppin' off on shit! You a lil gangsta," he pronounced, spinning around to face her.

"It's anythang for my nigga," she declared. Khalil laughed, then kissed her on the forehead.

"Oh, I'm yo' nigga nah? When we discussed that?"

"Not like that. Not like, boyfriend and girlfriend type shit, but like my nigga type shit. Like I'ma ride for you type shit, no matter who you wit'. Stop playin, you know the temperature," Janay explained.

"I know what'chu mean. You my nigga, too. I'ma ride for you too, lil fool," Khalil assured. Janay smiled before catching something out of her peripheral in the water.

"What the fuck?" she asserted. Khalil turned towards the creek and spotted what appeared to be a decomposed body. The head was missing, parts of the arms and legs as well, and the torso had been partially eaten.

"Look like a body," Khalil mentioned, flicking his roach to the ground.

"It is a body! Look, you can see the dick right there," she added. "Oh my God! This my first time seeing a body," Janay admitted.

"Come on, let's get the fuck from 'round here," Khalil insisted, grabbing Janay and pulling her towards the truck. They both hopped in and left the scene.

Chapter 17

(Class is In Session)

After Khalil dropped Janay off, he sparked another blunt and thought about the altercation at school. It baffled him how Janay popped off on his opps, but his brother didn't. Yeah, Kaleb pulled up to assist, but he didn't get active the way he should have. Khalil inhaled the high grade weed then exhaled slowly, shaking his head in disapproval. His phone rang moments later.

"Yo!" he answered.

"Damn, Killa, you forgot to call me?" Pimp inquired.

"Nah, big homie, I was headed to you now."

"Aight! I'm not home. Pull up on 25th Street, across from the Bails Bondsman," Pimp directed.

"You talkin' 'bout them apartments by the park?"

"Yeah! Pull in, then make that left. I'm at the last apartment on the right."

"Aight, I'm turning on Avenue I right nah," Khalil pronounced.

Khalil made a left into the apartment complex, made another left, and saw Pimp standing outside. Khalil hung the phone up and pulled up on Pimp. He parked and hopped out, dapping Pimp up.

"Wassup, Killa?" Pimp asked, smiling. "How was school? How did the lil eaterz react to you pullin' up in an

Aston Martin?" he asked curiously, rubbing his hands together. Khalil chuckled.

"It was kool, wassup, though? Why you wanted me to pull up?"

"Oh yeah, pull up," Pimp proclaimed, walking to the apartment that faced 25th Street.

"Yo' birthday next month, right? Dis yo' early gift. I wanted to get'chu outta yo' moma's apartment. This way, you ain't gotta worry about yo' moma hittin' yo' stash," Pimp explained, walking into the apartment. When Khalil walked in, the apartment was fully furnished. Both rooms had king-size beds with 70-inch screens, and the living room had a large sectional couch that wrapped around half of the living room, also with a 70-inch screen.

"Man, you fareal, Pimp?"

"You ain't neva gotta ask me that again. I'on play games, Killa. You my lil homie, my lil brother. I'ma always be here for you," Pimp assured. Khalil had to turn the other way and quickly swipe the tear that had cascaded down his cheek. No male figure had ever treated him with such love. After swiping the tear, he turned back towards Pimp and hugged him tightly.

"Thank you, my nigga. You a real one, man. I love you, fam," Khalil expressed.

"Love you too, Killa. Come on nah, we look out for each other. You shed blood for me. Can't get no deeper than that," Pimp retorted, unwrapping his arms from around Khalil. "Here!" Pimp said, handing Khalil a pair of keys. "This one is for yo' new apartment, and this one is for my house on Mayflower Street." Khalil grabbed the keys.

"Okay," Khalil replied, elated.

"Come on, follow me," Pimp insisted. Khalil followed Pimp to the back room. "Pull the cover back," Pimp said, smiling. Khalil pulled the cover back and spotted two small bricks.

"What's that?" Khalil asked, picking one up.

"When you was nowhere to be found, I hit them Haitians on Mayflower," Pimp informed. "That's two bricks of heroin."

"I don't know 'bout no heroin," Khalil admitted. Pimp smiled.

"Class is in session," Pimp asserted.

* * *

The next day after school, Khalil decided to let Marcia ride home with him. She had been texting him all day about it and after deciding between her and Janay, Khalil had chosen Marcia… even though he wanted Janay. He chose Marcia out of pity.

"Khalil?" Marcia called out.

"Yeah, wassup?" Khalil replied, bopping his head to the sounds of Big Khufu. Marcia turned the music all the way down to make sure she was being heard. Khalil gazed at her with a screw face.

"How you get a truck like this? What is you doin'? You don't even have a license, boy," Marcia pronounced with a nonchalant bluntness.

"Robbin' and killin'," he responded, then turned the music back up. Marcia turned it back down.

"Khalil, I'm serious!" He smiled before replying.

"My birthday in a few days. It was a gift. Nah, can I please listen to my music?" Marcia shook her head in disbelief and turned the sounds of Big Khufu back up.

"All in my DM's/ sayin' I'm a snake, nigga you trippin'/ Nawl, I'ma snake charmer/ lil nigga like an Egyptian/ we are not the same/ I be in them cars we different/ hop out do me/ hop back in nigga we shiftin'/ you the type/ to talk all that shit and get missin'/ I'm the type/ to spark on yo click and go to prison/ I'm the type/ to have all this motion without a deal/ say you shoot a nigga/ he ain't go under that's not a kill/"

Khalil vibed to the music in silence all the way to his apartment while Marcia gazed at him in deep thought.

* * *

Smack! Smack! Smack! Smack! Smack! Smack! Smack! The sounds of Khalil clapping Marcia's cheeks from behind reverberated with repetition throughout the apartment.

"Oh, my God! Khalil, wait!" Marcia cried, reaching behind her with her right arm, attempting to minimize the pressure that he was applying. Khalil grabbed her arm and pinned it behind her back, forcing her face to be pinned to the mattress. "Khalil!"

"Khalil, what? Huh?" Khalil asked. "This what'chu wanted, ana? Shut up and take it!" he barked through clenched teeth while proceeding to stroke her in a rabid frenzy.

"Sssss… oooow, fuck!" Marcia cried, her eyes rolling to the back of her head.

"Yeah, I know! Wet this dick up! Huh? Wet it!" Khalil yelled, never letting up the pressure. Moments later, he felt her vagina walls constricting around his dick. "Ffffuck! I'ma finna nut all in this pussy!" Khalil yelled, long stroking her viciously.

"Whooooooo… yesssss… baby!" Marcia cried as she came simultaneously with Khalil.

"Sshit!" he moaned, slowing his stroke while emptying everything he had into her canal. Marcia collapsed on the mattress, chasing her breath. When Khalil slipped out of her, he noted that he had blood and cum all over his dick and sheets.

"Fuck! Come on, get up!" he ordered, stepping out of bed.

"Hmmm… where we goin'? I'm sleepy," Marcia whined.

"We getting' in the shower. You got blood and nut all over my dick and sheets." Marcia sat up to examine her pussy, Khalil's dick, and the sheets.

"Oh my God! I'm so embarrassed. That's why I was tellin' you to step. You was hurting me," she complained, climbing out of bed.

"Did you nut?" Khalil asked with his brows raised. Marcia sucked her teeth.

"You know I did," she replied, wrapping her arms around him.

"Aight then! Nah, brang yo' ass on," he retorted, pulling her towards the shower.

Chapter 18
(Bitch Ass Nigga!)

Kaleb grabbed four tacos from out of Squeak's store behind 22nd Street and 23rd Street and headed back out front. Unable to wait until he got back home, Kaleb started demolishing the tacos in front of Squeak's store. Squeak was a well-known drug dealer who gave all the youngins a pack to get some money. He also was a known rat in the city. The Fedz had raided his store and confiscated over one-hundred bricks, a mixture of coke and heroin. After only a week in jail, Squeak was back out, and back to business like he never left.

"Say, youngin'!" Squeak called out. Kaleb turned towards Squeak with sour cream in the corner of his mouth.

"Yeah?" Kaleb retorted with a mouth full of food.

"Them tacos pressure, ana?" Kaleb shook his head up and down then proceeded to devour the tacos.

"Yeah, I know it!" Squeak boasted, then headed back inside his store / restaurant. Sccurrrrrrr!!!! Out of nowhere, a 2025 Branco pulled in front of Kaleb with three doors popping open, and three niggaz hopping out. Kaleb recognized all three of them, but not the fourth, who was the driver.

"Yeah, wassup nah, nigga?" Deon asked. "You bitch ass niggaz jumped me in school, wassup nah?"

"You know what it is!" Poodle added.

"Yeeaaaah!" Frank chimed in. Kaleb was terrified but concealed it.

"Do you, pussy!" Kaleb snapped, throwing his remaining tacos in Deon's face then rushing him with a two-piece combination. With sour cream in Deon's eyes, Kaleb was able to land both punches on his jaw and chin. Deon dropped to one knee. When Kaleb tried to advance, Poodle and Frank rushed him, peppering him with devastating blows dropping him. All Kaleb could do was ball up and try to protect himself.

"Beat that lil fuck nigga!" Rod, Deon's older brother, coached from the driver's seat. "Deon, get up and punish that lil bitch! You done let'em drop you! You better redeem yo'self!" Rod demanded. Deon joined in on the onslaught.

"Yeah, nigga, this 13th!" Deon bragged, kicking Kaleb in his head and face.

"Where yo' soft ass brother at nah? Huh?" Poodle asked, kicking Kaleb in the ribs and stomach.

"Fuck you, bitch ass niggaz," Kaleb spat even though he was in pain.

"Loc ass nigga!" Frank added, kicking Kaleb in the head.

Boc! Boc! Boc! Boc! Squeak let off four shots from SD, causing the trio to scatter back to the truck.

"Y'all get from in front of my store with that shit," Squeak demanded. "Rod, you know better! Get the fuck from 'round here!" Rod smiled.

"See you around, Squeak!" Rod lightweight threatened before pulling off.

"You alright, lil homie?" Squeak asked, bending down to examine Kaleb.

"Aaah! Fuck!" Kaleb cried, his face covered in blood.

Moments later, Khalil pulled up and hopped out to buy him some blunts. He'd just dropped Marcia off and was making a store run before going home. Khalil was about to enter the store when he glanced at someone bloody on the pavement.

"Da fuck?" Khalil muttered as he made his way towards the duo. "Kaleb, that's you?" When he noticed that it was his brother, he rushed over and kneeled beside him.

"Bra? What the fuck happened?" Khalil asked vehemently.

"It was them niggaz from 13th Street," Squeak explained. "I had to let off shots to get'em off of him."

"Get up! Come on!" Khalil remarked, helping Kaleb up. "Thank you, O.G.," Khalil told Squeak.

"Yeah, no problem. I know they'll prolly be back. I ain't worried though," Squeak enunciated. Khalil helped Kaleb into the front seat, then hopped into the driver's side and pulled off. Squeak noted how young Khalil was and the truck that he was driving. All of this piqued his interest, and he made a mental note to see exactly what Khalil was into. Back in the truck, Khalil was on the phone with Janay.

"Didn't you say yo' sister was a nurse?" Khalil questioned.

"Yeah, why?" Janay replied.

"I'm on my way! Tell yo' sister I'ma pay her to look at my brother!"

"Kaleb?"

"Yeah!"

"What happened?" Janay asked, worried.

"I'm finna pull up!"

"Okay!" Janay retorted. Click!

"Bra, talk to me! Who did it?" Khalil asked anxiously.

"Deon, Poodle, and Frank!" Kaleb replied, spitting up blood.

Khalil's vision turned bloody as he clenched his teeth and floored his truck.

Chapter 19

(Bed Rest)

When Latoya was done examining Kaleb, he had a gash over his right eye that needed stitches, a broken nose and two cracked ribs. Latoya was Janay's big sister and legal guardian, ever since their mother died.

"He'll be alright. Just make sure he gets at least three weeks of bed rest," Latoya suggested.

"I appreciate'chu, sis," Khalil mentioned, handing her five hundred dollars.

"No problem, anytime," she retorted, heading to her room.

"Three weeks bed rest? Nawl, man our birthday in a few days. I ain't tryin' to be laid up," Kaleb whined.

"Man, be quiet. You heard what she said, man. You got two cracked ribs. Lay yo' ass down," Khalil proclaimed. Kaleb sucked his teeth.

"Khalil, what happened?" Janay asked.

"Them niggas from school jumped Kaleb," Khalil explained.

"From 13th?"

"Yeah… Deon, Poodle, and Frank," Khalil added.

"Frank?" Janay's cousin who was seated at the kitchen table bagging up weed, asked.

"Who that?" asked Khalil.

"That's my cousin," Janay said.

"Yeah, Frank. Why, wassup?" Khalil asked. Janay's cousin got up from the table and approached Khalil.

"Wassup fam? I'm J-Fool," he said, extending his hand. Khalil glanced at Janay who shook her head in agreement.

"He solid," Janay assured. Khalil shook his hand.

"Where you from?" Khalil questioned.

"I'm from the 3," J-Fool admitted.

"Me too. Why I never seen you?"

"I just got out, fam," J-Fool added. Khalil nodded his head.

"So, what about Frank?" Khalil asked.

"Before I went in, I was at his top, you feel me? I been out two weeks, layin' on fool. He from 13th, but he got family in the B.G.'s (Bookers Garden). Every Sunday, he go to his people spot for a get-together, like Sunday dinner or some shit. Anyway, I'ma real gangsta fam, let me spin wit'chu," J-Fool pleaded. Khalil nodded his head while rubbing his chin, loving what he was hearing.

"What'chu want in for?" Khalil asked, lighting a pre-rolled blunt.

"A body, fam! I beat that shit, fam! All I do is get money and kill shit, fam," J-Fool enunciated with pride.

"I respect it," Khalil retorted, dapping up J-Fool. "J-Fool, huh?" Khalil mentioned, grinning.

"Yeah fam! Khalil, right?" J-Fool inquired.

"That's what the hoes call me. I go by Killa," Khalil pronounced.

"Say less, fam," J-Fool added.

* * *

A few days later…

"Happy birthday, daddy!" Janay sang cheerfully from the driver's seat, looking in the rearview mirror at Khalil who was in the back passenger's seat.

"Yeah, yeah," Khalil replied dryly, keeping his mind focused on what lie ahead.

“Chill out wit’ all that right nah, fam. We on somethin’,” J-Fool proclaimed from the passenger seat of the Benz he had rented. J-Fool and Khalil both had on Pooh Shiesty ski masks with ARPs in their laps. Janay just wore a hoodie.

“Okay, dang! Excuse me, then!” Janay shot back. Smoove shot her a look that said stop playin’ wit’ me. They were sliding down 27th Street when Lil Polo Da Don’s “Unnhmm” came on iHeartRadio.

“When I fuck her from the back, I be like Umm-hmm!” Janay sang. J-Fool quickly turned down the radio.

“Fam, this my last time tellin’ you, stop fuckin’ playin’ wit; me! You know that fuck ass jit don’t get no play in here! I’ma bag that jit when I catch’em! He can’t do no shows in the city! On Meezy, I’ma bag Polo soft ass! Nah, stop playin’ wit’ me and make that right, then that left in the B.G.’s” Janay smiled, knowing that Smoove hated Polo. She made a right on 27th and Avenue L, then made that first left into the two-story apartment complex.

“There that opp ass nigga right there, fam,” J-Fool stated, gripping his AR pistol. Khalil did the same as he embraced that adrenaline that real killers get before getting their man.

“Creep up and stop right in front of them,” Khalil suggested.

“Okay,” Janay repeated, pulling her hoodie low.

“Oooww, I got this fuck nigga nah,” Smoove muttered. When Janay stopped in front of Frank, he was laughing with his ten-year-old sister and a few of his cousin’s homies. J-Fool and Khalil’s doors opened, and they stepped out in unison. Without saying words, Frank’s cousin and his friend scattered for their lives, leaving Frank who didn’t run, alone with his sister.

“3 shit!” Smoove boasted, hitting Frank multiple times in the chest. They were amused at the way that Frank’s body jerked, resembling the dance known as the Nay Nay. When Frank dropped, Smoove stood over him and hit him all in the face. With no empathy, Khalil slayed Frank’s little sister.

Screams of terror could be heard while he stood over her body and watched it jerk from being riddled with bullets.

"Come on, fam!" Smoove pronounced, pulling Khalil by his shirt, snapping him out of a murderous trance. Khalil looked at Smoove, then looked at Frank who was already dead. He put two more holes in Frank, then hopped back in the Benz.

"Let's go, fam! Hit it!" Smoove demanded, tapping the dashboard.

Janay took them around the back of the complex and came out on 29th Street. She blended with traffic and headed to a bando where they switched tags and pulled the dark tint off. They then dropped the Benz off to J-Fool's mother, so she could take it back to be exchanged for another rental. After jumping in J-Fool's little Toyota Slider, they dumped the sticks in Taylor's Creek and headed back to Latoya's house to check on Kaleb.

Chapter 20

(First Blood)

When the trio entered the house, Janay headed straight to the showers, J-Fool sat at the kitchen table rolling up a blunt, while Khalil checked on Kaleb, who was in one of Latoya's spare rooms. Entering the room, Khalil found Kaleb gazing at the roof with one arm behind his head.

"Wassup, nigga?" Khalil asked, taking a seat in a La-Z-Boy that was next to the bed.

"Sup?" Kaleb asked dryly, still gazing at the roof.

"You ate?" Khalil asked, pulling at his phone.

"Latoya tried to feed me, but I told her I was straight." Khalil shook his head.

"You trippin'! I'ma order you Uber Eats," Khalil retorted, placing an order of Hungry Howie's Pizza. Kaleb inhaled deeply then exhaled loudly, agitated by the circumstances.

"Wassup?" asked Khalil.

"I'ma miss my first football game, and I'm laid up, all fucked up on my birthday and shit," cried Kaleb. Khalil jumped on Facebook, found the latest news and handed it to Kaleb.

"Happy Birthday, nigga," Khalil enunciated before pulling a blunt out and sparking it. Scrolling down Facebook, all Kaleb saw was R.I.P. Frank and Sweet Pea! Kaleb looked at Khalil then back at the phone. He tapped the screen and listened to a video that was posted.

"Oh, my God! They pulled up in broad daylight and just killed both of my kids! My baby girl was just ten years old, how could somebody be so treacherous?" cried Frank's mother. Kaleb passed Khalil back the phone aggressively.

"What the fuck is wrong wit'chu? A lil girl?" Kaleb lamented, a tear falling from one of his eyes. Khalil reached over and quickly wiped the tear from Kaleb's eye.

"All is fair in this game of murder. When it comes to vengeance, ain't no pickin' and choosing! You kill whoeva to cause pain… who EVA!" Khalil stated, getting up and heading towards the door. "Them niggaz coulda killed you, fool! Don't make me wish they should have! Tssss…!" Khalil hissed before walking out of the room and heading to the kitchen.

"I ain't gone lie, fam! We snapped! They goin' bray over Frank and his sister on the book," J-Fool boasted.

"I viewed that. Where Janay at?" Khalil asked.

"I think she still in the shower, fam."

"Aight," Khalil retorted, heading to the bathroom. The door opened when he twisted the knob. He entered and locked the door behind him. Janay peeped out of the shower.

"Hey, daddy," she said, smiling. "You finna join me?" Khalil said nothing while removing his clothes. He entered, grabbed the sponge from Janay and began to wash her back.

"You okay, baby?" she asked.

"How you feel, 'bout me killin' that lil girl?" Janay turned around to face Khalil, wrapping her arms around his neck.

"I'on feel no particular way about it. I understand when somebody draw first blood, anything goes. I understand where we live at, baby. You stood on bidness. Another bitch prolly wouldn't understand it, but I'm built different. Plus, I been in love wit'chu since the fifth grade." Janay expressed. She placed a tender kiss on Khalil's lips, then made her way down his chest, stomach and finally, slipping his dick into her warm wet mouth. Khalil respected Janay's answer, and truth be told, it made his feelings for her increase.

“I love you, too,” Khalil admitted. Hearing those words, Janay intensified the head she was giving… sending Khalil into a state of bliss.

Chapter 21

Soft and Cute)

Janay sat in her homeroom class, scrolling Facebook. She viewed all the grieving loved ones of Frank and his little sister Sweet Pea with stolidity. Janay felt no emotional attachment to the two deaths whatsoever. Sad to say… she was used to it.

"Janay! Put that phone away!" Mr. Solimene, who was at the chalkboard trying to teach Language Arts, demanded.

"Mr. Solimene, can I please be excused?" Janay asked.

"No, you may not!"

"It's that time of the month, it's urgent, Mr. Solimene. You understand that, right?" Mr. Solimene sucked his teeth.

"Ok, sure. You may be excused." Janay grabbed her Chanel backpack and headed out of the portable. When she made her way to the restroom, she ran into Poodle, who was leaving out of the male's restroom.

"Yeah, hoe! Wassup, nah? You all by yaself, nah! Talk that shit now, hoe!" Poodle dared, walking towards Janay.

"Go dig ya dead homie up, nigga!" Janay enticed, getting in his face.

"Hoe, I'll slap the shit outta you, bitch!" he threatened through clenched teeth.

"Nigga, you soft and cute, you just like a lil poodle," Janay added, smiling and pissing Poodle off all the more. Right when Poodle was about to swing, a teacher who was also taking a restroom break, called out.

"What are you two doing?" Ms. O'Brian asked.

"Nothing, just headed to the restroom." Poodle walked into the men's restroom and decided to wait on Janay to come out.

"I'm finna show this hoe. On Frank, I'm finna flush this hoe," Poodle muttered to himself before feeling a hand placed up under his chin. Khalil had been laying in the cut waiting to catch Deon or Poodle lacking. He had caught Poodle with his dick in his hand.

"Stupid nigga," Khalil pronounced, lifting Poodle's chin so that he could have access to the lower back of his head.

Khalil positioned the ice pick just at the base of Poodle's skull, slanted it upward, and slammed it directly into his brain. Poodle's eyes widened, he shook violently, then became still. Khalil was amused to hear his last breath release as a rattling-type sound. By leaving the ice pick in, there was little bleeding.

"Bitch ass nigga," Khalil spat, pulling Poodle into a stall and leaving him there. When he turned to leave, he noticed Janay standing in the doorway smiling. Khalil walked up on her and kissed her.

"Go back to class, I'll see you later," he promised, pulling his hoodie low and pulling his gloves off.

"Okay," Janay retorted, as she watched Khalil vanish from the campus. "Damn, I love that nigga," she whispered to herself, making her way back to class.

* * *

One month later…

Khalil was in the living room sitting on the couch next to Kaleb, scrolling Facebook and IG when his mother opened the front door and walked in. Penny hadn't seen Khalil since the day he had pistol whipped her, and she was looking forward to running into him.

"Well, I'll be damned! Look at what Satan dun dragged in!" Penny sputtered, placing her purse on the table, then placing her hands on her hips.

"Wassup?" Khalil asked, still trolling Facebook.

"Wassup? Wassup is, did you find them niggaz who jumped on yo' brother?" Penny asked, lighting a cigarette.

"Tsss… what'chu think?" Khalil shot back arrogantly.

"I'on think shit! But I know one muthafuckin' thang! You put that pistol upside my muthafuckin' head, you better damn sho' find them niggaz, and do the same!"

Khalil laughed then stood up.

"What'chu want to eat, bra?" Khalil asked Kaleb.

"Mirranda's! Philly cheese, extra onions and mushrooms, and get the bread toasted. Oh, and a blue Mystic," Kaleb said as his mouth watered, thinking about Mirranda's.

"Aight," Khalil retorted heading towards the door.

"Khalil, give me some money for my light bill," Penny begged. He stopped and gazed at his mother for a moment, then reached in his pocket and handed her five hundred dollars.

"Thank you, baby!" Khalil left without replying, jumped in his truck and left.

* * *

"Where you at, boy?" Janay demanded to know.

"I told ju bout that boy shit! I'm grown over here! Respect my maturity!" Khalil clowned.

"Nigga, you fourteen! You still got Carnation Milk on ya breath!" Janay shot back, laughing.

"Fuck you."

"Fareal, where you at?" She whined.

"I'm grabbin' Kaleb somethin' to eat."

"Oh. How he doin?"

"He better," Khalil retorted, spotting somebody of importance.

"That's good, tell him I asked about him."

"Yeah, aight! Aye, let me hit'chu back," Khalil said. Click!

Khalil put his food in the truck, then posted up, leaning on the front of it. Through the glass window he could see Tracy and her mother ordering food. Tracy was one of Khalil's Facebook friends. She was seventeen and wouldn't give Khalil the time of day claiming he was too young. After placing her order, she spotted Khalil through the window, waving her to come out. Tracy shook her head and told her mother she'd be outside. Stepping outside, the sun beamed perfectly off her high yellow skin with luminosity. She wore a Chanel legging suit that was so tight, it left little to the imagination. Thick in all the right places, Tracy had all the older niggaz wrapped around her finger.

"What up, lil boy? I told you, you is too young for me," she asserted with her hands on her hips and her camel toe protruding.

"What about this?" Khalil asked, pulling out a wad of all blue-faced, hundred-dollar bills. "How 'bout this?" he asked again, going into another pocket and doing the same. Tracy's pussy watered instantly. Khalil hopped into his truck and push started the Aston Martin.

"I guess I'm too young to be pushin' an Aston Martin too, huh?" Khalil proclaimed, smiling. Tracy walked over to the driver's side and peeped the inside. She had never ridden in an Aston Martin.

"Put my number in yo' phone, Khalil," Tracy remarked seductively.

"Oh, nah it's Khalil? I thought I was lil boy?" he clowned.

"I was just playin' wit'chu, baby," she lied, grabbing Khalil's phone and adding her number.

"Yeah, I know," Khalil said, grabbing his phone back.

"You gone get my nails done?"

"How much?"

"One-fifty."

“One-fifty, for some nails? Them bitches must gone be on yo’ hands for the rest of this year! That shit come wit’ a massage?” Khalil clowned. They laughed.

“Stop playin’ so much!” She chuckled. Khalil handed her four hundred dollars.

“Thank you! Call me tonight, my mama gone be gone to work,” Tracy mentioned with that “I’ma fuck you to death” look in her eyes.

“I got’cha!” Khalil assured.

“You promise?”

“Yeah, I got’cha,” Khalil retorted, peeling off.

Chapter 22

(That's Enough)

"Mmmmm… sssshit! Ssss… oooh, ffuck, Khalil! Khalil, what'chu doin' to me? Oh, my Gawd… yes!" Tracy yelled as Khalil punished her from behind. His roughness caused her head to hit the headboard occasionally, but Tracy didn't mind. She loved it.

"Sss… ooow, talk to me, daddy! Talk to me, while you get this pussy!" Tracy demanded through clenched teeth while gripping the sheets.

"Bitch, shut the fuck up and take this dick!" Khalil retorted, putting every muscle in his body into it.

"Ooow, fffuck, I'm nuttin'!" Tracy cried as she began to shake repetitiously. Before Tracy could get a full climax, Khalil snatched out of her.

"Sss… put it back in!" she cried. Instead, Khalil flipped her on her back. "Shit! That's what the fuck I want! Flip this shit!" she cheered on. Tracy grabbed both of her legs and put them behind her head, welcoming Khalil into her love pie. Boom! Boom! Boom!

"Bitch, who the fuck you got in there?" Tracy's brother yelled after banging on the door. Khalil swiftly wrapped his hands around Tracy's throat and proceeded to choke the very life from her. Her eyes bugged in confusion and terror as she began to kick and squirm, but to no avail. Khalil held a firm grip until Tracy was lifeless. Boom! Boom! Boom!

"Bitch, I know you hear me!" her brother continued. Khalil slid out of the bed quickly to put his clothes on, then went to unlock the door. The sound of the door being unlocked echoed loudly, then Tracy's brother twisted the knob and entered.

"Nawl, don't try to play sleep nah, hoe!" CRACK! Khalil smashed Deon in the back of the head, causing him to fall onto the bed.

"Aaah! What the fuck!" Deon cried, turning around while holding his head.

"Shut the fuck up, nigga!" Khalil demanded. When Deon saw that it was Khalil, he already knew what time it was.

"Aight man, don't shoot me… please!" Deon begged.

"I ain't gone shoot'chu, just get naked."

"What?"

"Fuck nigga, strip! Hurry the fuck up," Khalil threatened, cocking the hammer back for maximum intimidation.

"Aight!" Deon yelled frantically, snatching off all articles of clothing.

"Nah, I'm only gone tell you this one time. You play, I'ma blow yo' fuckin' head off! Understand?" Deon shook his head yes.

"Good. Nah, put that dick in yo' sister." Deon looked at his face with instant tears falling from both eyes. He knew Khalil was dead serious, so he climbed on top of his sister, inserted his dick, and began to pump away while crying. Khalil allowed two minutes to pass before intervening.

"Aight, nigga, that's enough. Turn over!" Deon did as he was told. Khalil grabbed him by his dreads, then placed the .40 up under his chin.

"That pussy was good, ana?" Khalil asked. Deon shrugged his shoulders with an awkward expression on his face, not knowing how to answer Khalil's question.

"It's okay, you can tell me," Khalil asserted, smiling demonically. Deon began to shiver in tears. Boc! Khalil hit Deon under his chin, splattering brain matter all over the headboard and abroad. He then put gloves on, wiped the gun, then placed it in Deon's hand. After wiping everything down, he left and slipped away unnoticed.

* * *

When Khalil pulled into his apartment, he noticed Pimp leaning on his scat smoking a blunt. Khalil killed the engine and stepped out.

“Wassup, killa?” Pimp greeted smiling. Khalil dapped Pimp up.

“Big homie, wassup wit’ it?”

“Aight… shit, just blowin’, waitin’ on you,” Pimp proclaimed.

“I’m here, what’chu need me or somethin’?”

“Nawl, just ain’t seen you in a lil minute!” Pimp added.

“Yeah, I been standin’ on a lot of bidness, lately,” said Khalil, crossing his arms across his chest.

“So, I hear.” Khalil gave Pimp a quizzical expression.

“Don’t look surprised, I keep my ear to the street. You did what you was supposed to do.”

“Fahsho,” Khalil remarked.

“You started movin’ that heroin yet?”

“Nawl, not yet,” Khalil responded.

“What’chu waitin’ on? Listen, you ain’t even gotta touch the shit. I know you got somebody you can trust. If not, get’chu a lil crew and make it happen,” Pimp schooled. Khalil listened intently.

“I hear you, Pimp.”

“Aight. Shid, what’chu did for your birthday?” Khali laughed.

“Stand on bidness!” Khalil retorted.

Chapter 23

(I'm So Sorry!)

Khalil was parked out in front of Marcia's house on 16th Street, smoking a blunt. She had been blowing his phone up, but Khalil kept leaving her on read, due to him having too much going on. He finally decided to pull up on her and check the temperature. The front door opened and Marcia came prancing out in a sundress that did little to hide her thick curves.

"Damn," Khalil mumbled to himself as she approached the truck. She opened Khalil's door with a smile on her face that stated she was happy to see him.

"What'chu doin' out here? I told you, the front door would be open. Why didn't you just come in?" Marcia inquired.

"I was just smokin', before I came in," Khalil responded.

"You coulda smoked inside."

"Yo' brother in there?"

"No, he with his girlfriend. Come inside," she pronounced, grabbing Khalil by the hand.

"Hold up!" he said, pulling his hand back. Khalil flicked the roach in the grass, grabbed his pistol then slid out of his truck, locking it.

"You don't need that over here, Khalil," Marcia stated solemnly.

"She go wherever I go," he retorted, tucking the pistol in his Celine's. Marcia shook her head and led the way into the house. This house was given to Marcia and her brother by their Jamaican father, who owned a lot of property. When

Khalil entered the house, he was instantly turned off at what he was seeing.

"Da fuck?" he said, a little louder than he meant. There was pizza boxes, Chinese food containers, soda cans, liquor bottles, cigarette butts, and cigar guts all over the living room table. PlayStation controllers and games were all over the floor, along with pairs of her brother's smelly shoes all over the place.

"You have to excuse my brother's mess. Him and his friend just messy," Marcia asserted, heading to her room. On the way to her room, Khalil noticed all the dirty dishes piled up in the sink and shook his head in disgust. As soon as he entered Marcia's room, he started to make an excuse to leave, but he knew she had missed him and decided to stay for a while. Heels and clothes littered the whole room and Marcia's bed sat on the floor without box springs or railings. Khalil thought, *how could a young woman as beautiful as she was, be so messy*?

"I was just about to clean right before you came," Marcia lied.

"Shid, you want me to leave so you can?" Khalil responded indignantly.

"Baby… don't do me like that. I promise, I'ma clean it when you leave," she asserted, wrapping her arms around Khalil's neck and placing a kiss on his lips. Khalil didn't kiss her back.

"Oh, nah you don't wanna kiss me?" She started kissing on his neck.

"Sshit!" he moaned.

"That's yo' spot, huh?" she asked, smiling before pulling her sundress over her head, dropping it next to scattered laundry. Biting her bottom lip, Marcia grabbed Khalil by his hand and backed her way up to the mattress.

"I want'chu to fuck the hell outta me," she requested, laying back on the mattress, and spreading her legs eagle. Gazing at Marcia's pretty pussy, Khalil noted how well-proportioned her vagina lips were, and how her clit sat perfectly in-between. He pulled a condom out, pulled it on, then placed his pistol next to the bed.

"This what'chu want?" he asked, pulling her to the edge of the mattress. He placed his forearms in the back of her knees, then lifted his arms, placing his hands around her neck. This position forced her feet to sit by her head. Marcia's pussy protruded out like a tropical papaya.

"Yes, I want it," she replied, already breathing heavily. Khalil navigated his pulsating dick to her wet and warm canal and slid in slowly.

"Mmmm!" Marcia moaned.

"Ffffuck!" Khalil added. He began to stroke her slow, long and deep, making a loud thud on contact each time. Marcia's walls began to tighten around his dick, causing Khalil to apply more pressure around her neck and turn his stroke game up. He was now slamming dick into her fast and violent. Marcia's eyes rolled to the back of her head, but she couldn't verbally scream because of how good it was due being choked.

"Yeah, yeah! Take this dick! Huh? Huh? This what the fuck you want?" Khalil asked aggressively through clenched teeth.

Every stroke that Khalil delivered, cum began to pour from Marcia's vagina profusely. In mid stroke, Khalil felt something slam on the back of his head and back. He instinctively rolled out of Marcia's pussy, grabbed his gun and turned to fire. Boc! Boc! Boc! Khalil looked around but saw no one.

"Khalil, what'chu doing?" Marcia questioned while catching her breath. "That was just my closet door. It's not on hinges, so I just lean it up against the wall. I can't believe you shot that gun in here," she added, a little scared and embarrassed.

"I can't believe how raggedy yo' fuckin' room is! I'm out!" Khalil snapped, snatching the rubber off his dick and throwing it in a pile of clothes. He pulled his pants back up and headed towards the door.

"Khalil, wait! Please, I'm so sorry—" Her words were cut off by the slamming of the door. Moments later, the sound of Khalil tearing the grass up while leaving echoed throughout the house. When Marcia finally made it to the door, Khalil was long gone!

Chapter 24
(Jumpman Krank)

"When I'm fishin' through yo' trenches/ AMG this bitch tinted

Niggas heard I'm tryna end'em/ So they say they gone surrender

I won't tell a soul when I get-em/ Nigga know that I'ma reaper"

J-Fool bobbed his head to the sounds of "Jumpman Krank" while smoking a 3.5 in a Grabba Leaf. He was backed in, behind tint at his apartment on 23rd and Avenue B with two AR pistols. One in his lap and one on the floorboard, both holding forty round clips. He also had Tisa in the car.

"You a fuck nigga!" Tisa snapped. J-Fool turned the music down.

"What?" he asked, blowing smoke from his nose.

"You heard me, nigga! You a fuck nigga!" she repeated more emphatically from the passenger's seat.

"Hoe, watch yo' fuckin mouth!" J-Fool snapped, dumping his blunt ashes on Tisa.

"Like I said! You killed my cousin, you a fuck nigga!" Tisa barked, not backing down.

"Hoe, you trippin'! You talkin' crazy!" J-Fool implied, grabbing his AR pistol.

"Whateva, bitch! You killed my cousin! Everybody know you did it, stupid nigga!" J-Fool lifted the baby stick, pointing it in Tisa's face.

"Bitch, I'll shoot'chu I yo' face, keep talkin' stupid! Bitch, you trippin!" Tisa smiled.

“You don’t scare me, nigga!” she admitted. J-Fool placed the ARP next to the one he had on the floorboard.

“Hoe, shut up and eat this dick!” J-Fool retorted, grabbing Tisa’s hair and placing her head in his lap. Tisa didn’t resist, she pulled his dick out and ate him up. Ten seconds into it, she pulled him out of her mouth.

“You still a fuck nigga,” she stated, then put him back in her mouth.

* * *

“Yeah, let me get ten of them steak tacos. Extra onion and cilantro,” Khalil ordered at Squeak’s store.

“I got’cha, young blood,” Squeak assured. “I need to holla at’chu before you leave too, young blood,” Squeak added.

“Killa!” Khalil retorted.

“Say what?” Squeak asked.

“You keep callin’ me young blood. My name is Killa,” Khalil informed, giving him the name Pimp gave him.

“Oh, okay! No problem, Killa. Let me chew some fat wit’chu before you leave.”

“Yeah!” Khalil replied, then his phone rang. “Wassup?” he answered.

“I’m down here. Where you at?” Erica asked.

“Where you at?”

“In front of the Substation.”

“Come down 23rd. I’m on Avenue E. You gone see my smoke gray truck parked at the store.”

“Okay, I’m coming now,” Erica said, hanging up. Moments later, Khalil spotted Erica’s Hellcat Durango. Hc waved his hand so that she’d see him. She made a left on Avenue E then made a right into Squeak’s store, parking next to Khalil’s truck. Khalil hopped in on the passenger’s side.

“Heeyy, daddy, I missed you,” Erica whined, leaning over to kiss Khalil on the cheek.

"You too," he replied.

"I like yo' truck."

"Yeah, yeah."

"Fifteen, no license, and gotta Aston Martin. You different," Erica complimented.

"You know it," Khalil responded nonchalantly. "Listen, I got the two ounces of coke for you. Just give me two bands," he said.

"Okay. Why do I feel like you got something else to tell me?"

"What'chu know 'bout heroin?" asked Khalil.

"I know about it. They love that shit on the reservation," she added.

"I came across a lil somethin'. You think you can move it?"

"Of course," she assured.

"Hold up," Khalil said before hopping out of Erica's truck. He grabbed a bag from his truck, then hopped back in with Erica.

"Here, this a whole brick."

"What'chu want for it?"

"Just bring me forty," Khalil pronounced, not caring about the price due to him acquiring it for free, and the fact that Pimp had showed him how to re-press them. He'd turned two into four.

"Forty? Shid, I got like… seventeen on me now," Erica proclaimed, reaching in her Birkin, pulling out the cash. She quickly thumbed through the money. "Yeah, that's seventeen," she assured.

"Okay, so that's fifteen on the brick and two for the two ounces? You owe me twenty-five bands," Khalil calculated.

"Okay, baby, no problem. Listen, I gotta go. I'ma call you when I'm ready."

"Fasho!"

"Be careful, Khalil," Erica stated before Khalil got out of her truck. He walked around to her side of the truck and kissed her on the lips.

"You know it," he replied, walking back into the store while she pulled off. When Khalil walked back into the store, he seen Squeak's wife serving a fiend from behind the counter. She flinched when she saw Khalil walk in.

"It's okay baby," Squeak assured, handing Khalil his food. "Let me talk to you outside." Khalil stepped outside, placed the food inside his truck, then grabbed his pistol and tucked it before closing the door. Khalil then stood in front of his truck.

"Wassup, old head?" Khalil asked.

"Squeak! They call me Squeak, Killa."

"Aight, Squeak. Wassup?"

"Look, I like how you move," Squeak admitted, eyeing Khalil's truck.

"Okay, and?" Khalil replied.

"What'chu into, if you don't mind me askin'?"

"I'ma all around street nigga. I'm on whateva," Khalil asserted.

"Shid… let me drop some work on you," Squeak suggested.

"Right nah, I'm good on that, but I'ma pull back up on you."

"Shid, get my number," Squeak pressed. Khalil stored Squeak's number in his phone then slid it in his pocket.

"Da fuck?" Khalil muttered. "Get down," Khalil yelled, pulling Squeak down in front of his truck. Boc! Boc! Boc! Boc! Shots rang from a Suburban. When Khalil rose and returned fire, he saw Rod clear as day. Rod sped off, but not before Khalil ran to the end of the street and let off four more shots, dropping the back window of the Suburban.

"Squeak, you good?" his wife Takesha asked from the entrance of the store.

"Yeah, baby, I'm good. Thanks to Killa," Squeak admitted, dapping Khalil up.

"Good lookin' Killa," Squeak pronounced.

"Thank you, baby," Takesha said, hugging Khalil.

"Who was that?" Khalil questioned.

"That was Rod. When them boys jumped yo' brother, he was wit'em. He was coaching them from the driver's seat. Baby, what's that boy name, who raped his sister then killed himself?" Squeak asked his wife.

"Deon!" Takesha answered.

"Yeah, Deon! Rod is Deon's older brother," Squeak stated.

"Oh, yeah?" Khalil replied, folding his arms across his chest. He silently praised himself for making it look like Deon had raped his sister before killing himself.

"I'ma get at'chu, O.G.," Khalil assured, hopping in his truck.

"Fasho, lil homie!" Squeak replied before Khalil pulled off. "I like that young nigga!" Squeak yelled.

Chapter 25
(F.S.G.)

Khalil had sent Marcia to voicemail for the eighth time. She had been blowing his phone up since the day he'd torn her grass up leaving her house.

"Damn, who keep blowin' up yo' line?" Janay asked, pursing her lips.

"Marcia," Khalil replied, waving his hand in a gesture of dismissal.

"Marcia?" J-Fool asked. "Marcia gotta brother named Kasper?"

Khalil shook his head yes.

"Why you wavin' yo' hand like she ain't nothin'? That's a baby, fam," J-Fool added.

"I'on even wanna get into that. We here on bidness!" Khalil asserted.

Janay smiled, elated that there was a bit of turbulence in Khalil and Marcia's relationship.

"Say less, fam," J-Fool pronounced.

"Your food's here," said the waiter, placing their plates in front of them filled with steaks, mac-n-cheese, and loaded potatoes.

"Thank you," Khalil asserted. The trio was having a meeting at Longhorn Steak House.

"Damn, this shit good," J-Fool mentioned.

"Umm-hmm!" Janay added.

"J-Fool, you know 'bout dog food?" Khalil asked.

"Of course, fam! It ain't too much I'on know about."

"Janay, you know 'bout molly?"

"No, but if you show me, I'ma take off," Janay replied, sure of herself.

"I'll show her, fam," J-Fool assured.

"Fasho! Don't sell nothin' less than an ounce," Khalil declared. "I'ma put'chu in a spot," Khalil added.

"I gotta spot, already, fam. Don't waste money getting' another one," J-Fool proclaimed.

"Where?"

"By the Family Dollar on 23rd and Avenue B. Janay, can move her sack in the spot too, so I can look after her," J-Fool suggested. Khalil shook his head in approval.

"J-Fool, I'ma give you a brick. Bring me forty. Janay, bring me ten."

"Got'chu fam. I got'chu, right nah, if you want it," Fool enunciated.

"Nawl, I'm good. I can wait," Khalil retorted. Listen, we don't do no tellin'! Remain forever solid, no matter what! From this day forward… we steppin' in the name of F.S.G.!"

"What's that, fam?" J-Fool asked.

"Foreva Solid Gangstaz!" answered Khalil. J-Fool and Janay both smiled.

"I like that!" Janay and J-Fool replied in unison.

"So, when we get this work?" J-Fool asked.

"Later on today," Khalil assured.

"May I help you with anything else?" the waiter asked.

"Yeah, let me get a take-out tray, please sir?" J-Fool asked.

"Sure thing," the waiter replied, leaving to grab the tray.

"Wassup?" Khalil asked.

"I gotta go take care of some bidness, fam. Hit me, if you need me."

"Here's your tray, sir," the waiter said, handing J-Fool the tray. J-Fool loaded the food into the tray.

"I'ma take care of the bill," Khalil told the waiter. "Come back in fifteen minutes." The waiter left with the promise of returning.

"Aight fam, F.S.G.!" J-Fool stated before leaving.

"Foreva solid!" Khalil retorted. Janay waited until J-Fool left before asking Khalil something important.

"Khalil, you know them krackaz asked me about Poodle?" Janay mentioned, digging in her loaded potatoes.

"What they talkin'?"

"A teacher seen me and Poodle talkin' before he died. They just asked me did I see anything. I told them no and that I just used the restroom and left. I told them that I was glad I didn't see shit, kuz the killa prolly would of killed me too," Janay remarked with a chuckle.

"Good!" Khalil said, stuffing steak in his mouth.

"You heard what happened to Deon and his sister Tracy?" Janay asked.

"Nawl, what happened?" Khalil lied.

"He raped his own sister, then killed hisself! That nigga must have been flock, kuz ain't no way," Janay voiced.

"Damn, that's crazy! He went out like that? He lucky he killed hisself before I got to his ass," Khalil laughed sinisterly, silently brimming with self-adulation at how brilliantly treacherous he was.

Chapter 26
(Need Some Help?)

"Wassup bra, you good?" Khalil asked Kaleb over the phone while parked out front of Marcia's house.

"Yeah! About another week or so, I'll be able to go back to football practice. I went back to school today. Maan! I heard Poodle got killed in the restroom, and Deon raped his own sister, then committed suicide! It's some weird shit goin' on bra, fareal!" Kaleb stated.

"I'on feel no empathy for none of them niggaz. Fuck'em!" Khalil replied.

"Shid, I'm wit'chu! Fuck'em! Shit just weird to me," Kaleb voiced.

Marcia walked out of her house, looking devastatingly beautiful.

"Aye, bra. I'ma hit'chu later. You need somethin'?"

"Nawl, I'm good," Kaleb assured.

"Aight!" Click! Khalil hung the phone up as soon as Marcia reached the passenger side pf his truck. She opened the door and hopped in.

"Hey, Khalil," Marcia greeted, knowing what kind of mood Khalil was in.

"Wassup?" he replied dryly.

"Why you been ignoring my calls?" she whined, turning in her seat to face him. Khalil exhaled before replying.

"Look, my nigga. I fuck wit'chu! I been fucked up bout'chu, since sixth grade. You always been beautiful, you always dressed to kill, so you threw me off when I seen how dirty yo' house was. You coulda at least had yo' room clean," Khalil explained.

"I know, I was so embarrassed, but it's clean now. I cleaned the whole house."

"That's good. What about the closet door?" Marcia shook her head no.

"It's still off the hinges," she admitted shamefully. Khalil instantly went in his pocket, pulled out and peeled four hundred dollars off, handing it to Marcia. Her eyes lit up.

"Khalil, you didn't have to do that," she stated, grabbing the money.

"That shit ain't 'bout nothin'," he flexed. Marcia gazed at Khalil for a moment.

"Kahlil, what'chu do for money?" Khalil looked her in the eyes.

"Whateva," he responded seriously. Marcia continued to stare at him with admiration.

"You wanna come in?"

"Nawl, I can't. I just stop by to check on you. I gotta go handle some bidness," Khalil proclaimed, looking out of his window, spotting a familiar face across the ditch on the same street as Marcia's.

"Can I go wit'chu? Please?" she begged.

"Not this time." She sucked her teeth.

"Look, I gotta go," Khalil stated while taking a peek across the ditch to keep an eye on the subject.

"Khalil, what we doing? What is this between me and you… like… am I yo' girl or what?" Marcia vented.

"We'll revisit the convo' another time. I gotta go!"

"You prolly finna go see that bitch, Janay!" she snapped.

"Listen, don't eva in yo' life, call Janay outta her name! She ain't did a fuck thang to you!" Marcia's eyes widened with anger and surprise.

"The same shit go for her too! She can't say shit bout'chu in front of me! You understand me?" Khalil snapped. Marcia's feelings were conflictual. She was angry, shocked, and turned on all at once.

"Yes!" she replied, while exiting the truck wit' tears in her eyes.

Khalil quickly backed out of her yard and made his way across the ditch, creeping past the familiar face's yard.

"Well, looky here, looky here," Khalil sang, watching his target go inside his house. Khalil picked his phone up and dialed out. The receiver picked up on the second rang.

"I need ju, fam," Khalil remarked.

"Whateva, fam!" J-Fool retorted.

"You gotta murder bucket?"

"Stay wit' one, fam, stop playin'!"

"I'm finna pull up."

"I'm on the 3!"

"Say less!" Khalil replied. Click!

* * *

Khalil had J-Fool trailing his victim while he sat anxiously in the passenger seat, ready to get active. They followed the mark to a rundown motel on 20th Street called Renos. Once he went inside, Khalil had J-Fool to park directly next to his Audi and popped the trunk. Khalil gave the front tire on the driver's side a flat, then got back in the murder bucket and waited. One hour and six blunts later, the mark finally came out and noticed the flat tire instantly. He cursed the Gods, then popped his trunk and grabbed a spare and a jack. Khalil slipped out of the passenger's seat and crept up on the mark, who was busy taking the lugs off.

"You need some help, buddy?" Khalil asked, startling the guy.

"Nawl, I got it, thank you."

"Okay," Khalil replied, snatching a big chrome .40 from his hoodie and whacking the mark across his bald spot in the crown of his head. Before the mark dropped, J-Fool was already out of the car, helping Khalil pistol whip him.

"Drag this fuck nigga to the truck," Khalil demanded. They tucked their guns, dragged him to the back of the car, then threw him in. Khalil duct taped his mouth while J-Fool tied his hands behind his back, and his feet together. Khalil spit on the mark before closing the trunk. They both hopped back in the bucket and J-Fool pulled off. Khalil's phone rang moments later.

"Yo'?"

"Heyy, baby! I'm done with that. I'm about to get on the road to come see you," Erica stated.

"Nawl, don't go nowhere! I'm on my way to you," Khalil stated.

"That's even better! See you when you get here, daddy!" Erica retorted. Click!

"Aye fam?" J-Fool asked.

"Yeah?"

"Who in the trunk?"

"One of my moma's ex boyfriends. Fuck nigga used to torture me," Khalil revealed.

"Oh yeah, we finna punish him, fam! Where we headed?"

"Take Okeechobee Road all the way out. We headed to the Indian reservation." Khalil had just kidnapped Cecil. When he was younger, he vowed to kill him when he got older and now, the universe had conspired with him for retaliation.

Chapter 27
(I'm Saved)

Two and a half hours later, J-Fool was pulling into Erica's massive home. She was outside, smoking a cigarette laced with coke and sipping Don Julio.

"Damn, who big sexy is?" J-Fool asked putting the car in park. Khalil chuckled.

"That's my home girl, slash smash every nah and again," Khalil replied.

"Okay, say no moe. Wassup wit all these foreigns and four-wheelers and shit?"

"This how they livin' out here. Step out," Khalil asserted. When they stepped out, Erica met them halfway.

"Hey daddy," she greeted, kissing Khalil on the lips.

"Wassup, E?"

"Who you got wit'chu?"

"This my nigga, J-Fool. J-Fool, this Erica," Khalil introduced.

"Nice to meet'chu, J-Fool," she greeted, shaking his hand.

"You too, miss," J-Fool replied. Erica laughed.

"Miss? Boy, I'm not that old. You can call me Erica," she suggested, pulling from her cigarette.

"Okay, Erica," Fool added.

"So… wassup, daddy? I know you ain't come way out here in these woods just to see me. So, wassup?" asked Erica.

"I gotta nigga in the trunk," Khalil admitted.

"Nha-uhha! Let me see!" she pronounced, flicking the cigarette butt. Khalil walked her to the back of the car.

"Pop the trunk, Fool!" Khalil requested. J-Fool popped the trunk, then joined them behind the car. Erica's eyes widened with excitement.

"Damn! What the fuck he did to end up in the trunk?" Cecil was squirming and attempting to cry for help, but the duct tape muffled it.

"This fuck nigga abused me when I was a kid?" Khalil pronounced.

"Sexually?"

"Fuck no! Bitch ass nigga used to beat the shit outta me." Khalil closed the trunk.

"Oh yeah, he deserve to be in there. So, why you brought him here? You wanna leave'em in the woods?" Erica asked out of curiosity.

"Nawl, I wanna put his ass in that tank!" declared Khalil.

"Khalil! I can't believe you risked driving way out here with a body in the trunk, just to put him in the tank. You could of put'em in Taylor's Creek," Erica stated, laughing. "Roll around back, I wanna see this shit," she admitted, making her way around back.

"Tank? What tank, fam?" J-Fool asked.

"In the back," Khalil informed, getting in the driver's seat, while J-Fool hopped in the passenger seat.

"What's in the tank, fam?" J-Fool asked. Khalil smiled and drove around back.

"Get out," Khalil told J-Fool after popping the trunk.

"What the fuck? Fam, she really gotta tank wit' gators in it in her backyard? She snapped fam!" J-Fool expressed.

"Help me get this nigga out the trunk!" Khalil enunciated.

J-Fool made his way to the trunk and helped Khalil pull the body out.

"You need anything?" Erica asked.

"Yeah! Let me get some rope, a huntin' knife, and a road flare if you got one," Khalil pronounced.

"I got all that!" she said, leaving to go get what she was told.

"Fuck you finna do? Let's just put his ass in there, fam," J-Fool suggested, ready to see the gators put in work.

"Shit deeper than that!" Khalil responded.

"Here, daddy!" Erica said, handing Khalil the tools. Khalil grabbed the hunting knife and began to cut away all Cecil's articles of clothing. When Cecil was naked, Khalil grabbed the rope.

"Help me, drag this nigga to the palm tree, by the tank."

J-Fool gave Khalil a hand, dragging Cecil to the tree and tying him to it. Khalil then squatted in front of Cecil and removed the duct tape from his mouth.

"Please, man! Don't kill me!" Cecil begged frantically.

"Nigga, shut the fuck up!" J-Fool snapped, placing his pistol on the side of Cecil's head.

"You know who I am?" asked Khalil.

"Yes! I do, but Khalil, I'm saved now! I'm a Christian man! I'm sorry for what I did to you!" Smack! J-Fool smacked Cecil in his mouth with the gun, busting it up.

"My nigga don't wanna hear that fuck shit!" J-Fool added. Khalil pulled his pistol out.

"J-Fool, turn yo' head for a minute," Khalil advised. J-Fool turned away. "Open yo' mouth, nigga!"

"Come on, man!" Cecil cried.

"Last c chance," Khalil warned through clenched teeth. Cecil complied, opening his mouth. Khalil pulled his dick out and pissed in Cecil's mouth.

"Drink it, bitch nigga!" Cecil took periodic gulps of Khalil's piss until he was done.

"What the fuck you on, fam?" J-Fool asked. Khalil shook his dick, then put it back in his pants.

"You good, bra. Turn around," Khalil said, putting the tape back on Cecil's mouth. "This fuck nigga used to beat me and make me suck my sheets when I pissed in the bed." J-Fool hit Cecil three more times in the face with his pistol, breaking his nose and knocking one of his eyes from its socket.

"Fuck his ass up!" Erica cheered, then took a hit of coke. Khalil grabbed the road flare and set it off. He then placed it under Cecil's balls and set them ablaze. The pain was so unbearable that Cecil passed out. Khalil grabbed the hunting knife and watched it cut through his balls like butter. This caused Cecil to wake back up and make muffled sounds. Khalil showed him his balls, then threw them in the tank. He then cut slabs of flesh from Cecil's arms, legs, and torso, throwing all of it in the tank.

"Aight, that's enough of this shit! Help me put this nigga in the tank," Khalil said, untying Cecil.

"'Bout time, fam!" J-Fool stated, helping Khalil put Cecil in the tank. The gators hadn't eaten in a while, so they ravaged Cecil's body until he was no more.

Chapter 28
(Just Fall Back!)

Two weeks later…

Khalil was backed in at J-Fool's spot on 23rd and Avenue B, with Kaleb in the passenger seat watching all the motion. He had told J-Fool to sell his ounces of heroin for a thousand, and for Janay to sell her ounces of molly for two hundred. Lowering the prices had traffic in and out, causing the work to dwindle quickly.

"Damn, this shit swangin'!" Khalil said out loud to no one in particular. His phone rang moments later.

"Yeah, wassup?" he answered.

"Hey, Khalil. What'chu doing?" Marcia asked.

"I'm outside, wassup?" Before she could answer, J-Fool was tapping on Khalil's window.

"Hold up," he told Marcia, letting his window down.

"Wassup, Fool?" Khalil asked.

"This shit finna be gone, fam! We need moe work!" J-Fool declared.

"I'm on top of it, give me a lil minute," Khalil proclaimed, holding the phone away from his ear.

"Aight, fam. Foreva solid!" J-Fool replied.

"Death and beyond," Khalil retorted before J-Fool spun off. "Yeah, wassup," Khalil spoke into the phone.

"Yeah! Khalil, I was calling you, because I forgot to ask you, if you heard about Frank, Poodle, Deon and his sister?" Marcia asked.

"You really hit my line 'bout that shit?"

"Aahh… yeah. That was messed up right?" she pried.

"So, I'm supposed to feel some type of empathy for opps?"

"I… I was just—"

"Listen, don't ever call my phone wit' that fuck shit, again!" Click! Khalil hung up on Marcia, then put his truck in drive. "Hold it down, I'll be back!" he yelled out to J-Fool then pulled off.

"Bra, I want in!" Kaleb declared.

"In on what?" Khalil asked glancing at Kaleb, then back at the road in front of him.

"Put me on, I'm tryna eat, too!" Kaleb stated seriously. Khalil laughed at his brother's request. "The fuck is so funny?" Kaleb snapped.

"Yo, man! I'm not puttin' no work in yo' hand! Just fall back! If you need somethin', bitch, I got'chu!" Kaleb sucked his teeth.

"You put work in that nigga J-Fool hand! That bitch Janay too!" Kaleb snapped.

"First off, don't ever disrespect Janay again! You gone respect her, nigga! Especially after she put that work in for you, nigga! And secondly, you ain't built for what come wit' this shit! So, you can fall back, and get free bandz… or fuck ya, nigga! But what'chu not gone do is disrespect nobody on my team!" Khalil enunciated, pulling into Squeak's store and putting his truck in park. Kaleb batted the air with his hand.

"Yeah, whateva," Kaleb stated. Khalil went in his pocket, pulled out a hand full of blue-faced hundreds, and threw them in his brother's face before walking off.

"Yeah, okay," Kaleb muttered, picking the money up. As soon as Khalil walked into the store, Takesha lit up, smiling irrepressibly.

"Heeyy, Killa," she spoke seductively.

"Wassup, man. How you?" Khalil replied, looking *fway* with his designer and jewels on.

"I'm just koolin', you know, slow motion," she declared.

"Fasho!"

"You hungry?" she asked, putting the finishing touches on a blunt that she was rolling.

"No, thank you. I'm here for Squeak," he responded.

"Squeak!" she yelled. Moments later, Squeak came from an office in the back of the store. "Killa here for you," Takesha pronounced, putting flame to her blunt.

"Killa! What the lick read?" Squeak greeted, dapping Khalil up.

"We need to talk."

"Shid, talk!" Squeak chortled, folding his arms across his chest.

"Here?"

"Yeah! My wife thorough," Squeak assured. Khalil glanced at Takesha, who had on a ton of gold from her neck to her fingers, then back to Squeak.

"I need some work," Khalil remarked. Squeak nodded his head up and down.

"Up front or the back end?"

"I'ma hit'chu on the backend, O.G.," Khalil replied.

"What'chu want?"

"Boi and molly."

"Shid… what'chu can handle?" Squeak pressed.

"Whateva!" Khalil assured.

"Say less!" Squeak muttered with elation, delighted to have a YN of Khalil's caliber under his wing. "Bring me seven for the molly and fifty for the boi," Squeak stated.

"Overstood," Khalil replied.

"Where you gone be in an hour?" Squeak asked, checking his AP.

"I'ma be around."

"Text me where you want'em at, and I'ma have Takesha drop'em off," Squeak announced.

"Fasho!" Khalil retorted.

* * *

When Khalil pulled in front of his mother's apartment, Kaleb got out and headed inside. He had been silent the whole ride from Squeak's store. Khalil killed the engine and headed inside behind him. He spotted Pimp in the living room, sitting on the couch with his mother. Kaleb headed upstairs.

"Wassup Killa?" Pimp spoke. Penny's face formed into an expression of confusion.

"Wat up, Pimp!" Khalil retorted.

"Killa?" Penny asked.

"You know what's goin' on," Khalil stated arrogantly. Penny shook her head in disbelief.

"Come on, let's step out," Pimp suggested, heading outside. Khalil threw a couple hundred on the couch, then followed Pimp outside.

"What'chu been up to?" Pimp questioned.

"Grindin'! Got me a lil team, like you suggested. They gotta spot on the three doin' numbers! Work already gone," Khalil asserted.

"You need moe work?" Pimp asked, his eyebrows raised.

"Not right nah. I already gotta lil play in motion."

"From who?"

"Some old nigga, name Squeak," Khalil pronounced.

"Squeak?" Pimp asked.

"Yeah!"

"Squeak, who own the store on Avenue E?"

"Yeah!"

"Fffuck!" Pimp impulsively shouted.

"Wassup?" Khalil asked, his expression studious.

"Maan… that nigga the police!" Pimp expressed, mad that Khalil had allowed himself to be lured into Squeak's snake-like suavity.

"Oh yeah?" Khalil replied dryly, not really caring about Squeak's situation.

"Yeah! Cut all ties with that nigga, ASAP!" stressed Pimp.

"Say no moe!" Khalil replied to Pimp, but already had it embedded in his mind to get the work from Squeak and buck him.

"I'ma go see that 'bout that shit! Nawl, I'ma kill that bitch ass nigga!" Pimp spat heatedly.

"Nawl, Pimp! Me and my team got it. Don't trip!" Khalil assured.

"Aight nah! Y'all handle up or I'ma do me," Pimp promised.

"I hear you!" Khalil replied.

Chapter 29

(Love You Too)

Daylight was beginning to fade when J-Fool was on 23rd in front of the spot, leaning in the passenger's window of Tisa's sister's car.

"Give me some money for my phone bill and nails," Tisa lightweight demanded J-Fool.

"Shid… you gone eat me up later?" J-Fool asked, smiling devilishly.

"Uh-uhh, boy, don't talk to my sister like that," Andrea asserted. Andrea was Tisa's older sister.

"You want'cha phone bill and manicure too?" J-Fool asked Andrea.

"Hell, yeah!" she replied, smiling.

"Well, shut the fuck up! Tisa know what's goin' on!" J-Fool snapped.

"Lil boy, you just too damn much! Too much for ya damn self," Andrea added. J-Fool threw a thousand in the car window.

"That's five hunnid a piece! Y'all burn rubber, you makin' the spot hot! Tisa, hit me later," Fool pronounced, backing away from the car.

"Okay!"

"Thank you, wit'cha disrespectful ass!" Andrea added, pulling off.

* * *

"Hey, daddy!" Janay answered her phone.

"Wassup, J? You good, you need anything?" Khalil asked.

"Aight."

"What J-Fool doin'?" Janay got up to look out the window.

"He outside in his phone," she stated, closing the curtain.

"Aight, I'll just bring him the same shit," Khalil proclaimed.

"Did the package make it there yet?"

"Yeah, like thirty minutes ago," Janay retorted.

"Fasho! I'll be through there," Khalil promised.

"Okay, daddy." Click! Janay hung the phone up then looked out of the window again.

Boc! Boc! Boc! Boc! Boc! Boc! Boc!

"J-Fool!" Janay yelled, running out of the room. She grabbed a Blackout 300 from the couch in the living room, then ran outside. The shooter was gone, while J-Fool was rolling, putting pressure on his stomach.

"J-Fool!" she yelled rushing to his aid.

"Lock the trap up and put me in the car. Take me to Lawnwood I can't wait for no ambulance," he stated through clenched teeth.

"Okay!" she replied, taking the rifle back inside and locking the spot up. She then grabbed his keys, money, and phone.

"You need help?" a man walking by asked.

"Yeah, help me get him in the car," she pleaded. The stranger helped put J-Fool in the back of his car then left. Janay jumped in the driver's side and headed to Lawnwood, doing the dash. When she pulled up, there were EMT's already outside.

"Help, I need help!" she cried frantically, covered in blood.

One EMT ran to get a stretcher.

"What happened?" asked the medic.

"I don't know! I found him on the side of the road! I think he's been shot!" Janay pronounced. The other medic came back and helped the other put J-Fool on the stretcher.

"What's his name?"

"I don't know," Janay replied, before hopping in the car and pulling off. When she was pulling out of the hospital, she dialed Khalil's number.

"I'm on my way to the spot nah!" he stated.

"J-Fool been shot!" Janay disclosed painfully, tears falling from her eyes.

"What?" Khalil snapped.

"I just dropped him off to Lawnwood! I left so they won't ask me no questions!"

"What about the spot?"

"I locked it up! I told them I found him on the side of the road, so they wouldn't send them krackaz to the spot!"

"You did good! How he lookin'?"

"He was still conscious, but I'on know! He got hit like seven, eight times!" she replied.

"Fffuck! Aight, go grab everything out the spot and take it to my apartment."

"Okay, Khalil, I love you!"

"Love you, too!" Click!

* * *

One week later…

Khalil and Janay were keeping J-Fool company in his room at Lawnwood Medical with boxes of pizza and perk 30'2. He had been hit seven times without damaging any real organs.

"Wassup my nigga, how you feelin'?" Khalil asked, biting into a slice of pizza.

"Shid, I'm feelin' like getting' my lick back! That's all I been thinkin' 'bout, fam," J-Fool vented.

"Say less, bra! You already know that's automatic. I'm askin' you, how you feelin'?"

"I'ma gangsta, fam! I ain't doin' no trippin, I'm good, fam!" J-Fool assured.

"Fasho! You know who hit'chu?"

"Nawl. I had my back turnt, fam, but like I said, I'm trippin! I'm standin on big bidness! I'm finna terrorize everything, fam!"

"You know I'm wit'chu," Khalil added. J-Fool nodded his head up and down.

"Janay, fam, I love you. You saved my life," J-Fool pronounced.

"Love you too, kuz," Janay retorted.

Chapter 30

(Young Nigga World)

It was 12:30 in the morning and the crowd in front of The American Legion was thick and boisterous. Men of all ages made passes at Latoya, but she turned them all down. After downing two blue Long Island iced teas, she decided that it was time to go. On her way out of the club, the bouncer at the door couldn't keep his eyes off her curvaceous frame and meaty camel toe.

"You leaving already?" asked the bouncer, grabbing at his dick and licking his lips. Latoya closed the space between them, rubbed him on his bald head, and licked his ear.

"Yeah, this is it for me," Latoya chortled, then walked away making her ass clap excessively. Not looking back, she headed straight to her car, unlocked it and got in. After trying to start the engine several times, she popped the hood and meddled with the battery cables.

"Damn, thickness… you need some help?" a man asked who was on his way to his car. Latoya turned to see who had offered help.

"No, thank you! My nigga on his way," she replied, turning back around to look under the hood with her ass tooted up.

"You sho'?"

"Look, man, get the fuck on!" she snapped.

"Well, fuck you then, bitch!" the man retorted before walking away.

"Yeah, I know," Latoya added, not looking behind her.

"Don't pay him no mind. He a bug," the bouncer stated. Latoya turned and saw that it was the bouncer.

"I know, right! Gotta nerve to cuss a bitch out kuz I'on want his help."

"Fuck him! Wassup though? You mind if I take a look?" he asked. Latoya looked behind her then backed up, purposely putting her big soft ass cheeks on his dick.

"Excuse me, I'm sorry," she remarked, seductively moving to the side.

"You good," he assured, sneaking in a squeeze of her ass cheeks.

"I think it's my starter," she mentioned at the same time as her phone rang. "Excuse me, I gotta take this call," Latoya asserted.

"Aight, handle ya bidness," he declared, taking a look under the hood.

Latoya disappeared to take her call.

"Oh shid… her battery cables loose," he mumbled to himself. Moments later, Rod felt the undeniable feeling of steel being placed in the back of his head. Before he could react, Janay put one in his head, slumping him under the hood. She took off immediately afterward. J-Fool and Khalil materialized from behind a SUV and let two 300 Blackout's go, peppering his body with 223 rounds efficiently. Rod was already dead before his riddled body twisted, spun, and hit the ground in front of the totaled vehicle. The duo disappeared unnoticed due to everyone being inside the club. They hopped in a getaway car, where Janay and Latoya were waiting and slipped away, under the Florida moon.

* * *

The next day, Khalil pulled up to Squeak's store and hopped out with four pockets full of paper. When he entered the store, Takesha was at the register smoking a blunt as usual.

"Wassup, Killa?" she spoke. Takesha was a pretty, big-bodied woman with a lot of ass. She was also tatted up and dipped in the finest gold and diamonds.

"Slow motion," Khalil responded.

"You want Squeak?"

"Shid, I rather have you, but that can wait," Khalil remarked, shooting his shot for shock value. Takesha smiled shamelessly before replying.

"You is not ready," she mumbled loud enough for Khalil to hear. "Squeak!" she called out.

"Jump out there," Khalil dared. Takesha nodded her head okay. Moments later, Squeak emerged from the back of the store.

"Main man, Killa! What the lick read?" he asked, dapping Khalil up. Khalil pulled thirty thousand from his left pocket and handed it to Squeak. Takesha smiled, admiring the young bull. Khalil pulled out a chrome and black .380, placed it on the ice cream cooler, then pulled out twenty thousand from his right pocket and began to count it.

"That mothafucka pretty," Squeak pronounced, picking the gun up to examine it.

"Here. Altogether, this fifty thousand. I owe you sixty-four," Khalil calculated for two bricks of heroin, and two bricks of molly.

"I ain't trippin'! You coulda waited until you finished everythang," Squeak stated, handing Khalil back the pistol.

"Just wanted you to know I ain't playin'," Khalil retorted, tucking the pistol.

"I hear you," added Squeak.

"Listen, I gotta shift. I'ma fuck wit'cha, O.G.," he said, dapping Squeak up before turning to leave.

"Fuck wit' me," Squeak replied, heading towards the back.

"Aight, Takesha. I'ma see you, later."

"Make sho' you do," Takesha replied before Khalil slipped outside.

Khalil jumped in his truck, put the pistol in a shoe box next to some money, then pulled his gloves off.

"I ain't payin' you shit else… and I'ma fuck yo' bitch, old ass nigga. This a young nigga world," Khalil said aloud to himself before turning up YNW Melly's "Murda On My Mind" and pulling off.

Chapter 31
(I Gotta Tell You Somethin')

It was a nice balmy Saturday at 13th Street football field. The sun wasn't blazing hot, and a light breeze saturated the atmosphere while family and friends cheered for their teams. Steppaz and beautiful women of all ethnicitics from all sides of town were gathered around the field, so tension was thick. Pimp was yelling and moving back and forth every time Kaleb gained yardage on a play, while Khalil, J-Fool, and Janay paid attention to their surroundings.

"I know I'ma have to kill one of these niggaz out here in broad day, fam," J-Fool declared seriously.

"I know. I feel the same way, gang," Khalil retorted.

"We playin' it real close behind enemy lines," Janay added.

Khalil nodded his head in agreement.

"Fuck it, we out here nah," Khalil assured.

"Let's go! That's what the fuck I'm talking 'bout! Get in that box, lil nigga! I gotta thousand for you if you get in that box, Kaleb! Let's fuckin' go!" Pimp barked.

The quarterback yelled, "Hut," then threw Kaleb a twenty-eight pitch. Kaleb cut to the right with the fullback blocking every defensive player that attempted to tackle Kaleb, clearing a path all the way down the sideline. When Kaleb reached the endzone, the crowd went wild, while he did the "Stan the Man" dance.

"That's my lil nigga! They can't fuck wit'chu! I gotta band for you, lil nigga! Yeah!" Pimp yelled, clapping his hands aggressively.

"Yeah! Aye, y'all hold it down. I'm finna run to the car right quick! I want him to have this money, soon as he come off the field," Pimp stated, trotting off. After a few minutes ticked by, Khalil gave J-Fool a direct order.

"Aye, Pimp trippin', go make sho' he good," Khalil suggested. J-Fool quickly made his way to the entrance. As soon as he made it out the gate, shots rang out. Boc! Boc! Boc! Boc! Boc! Boc! Boc! Boc! Boc!

The piercing sound of a biometric trigger echoed throughout the atmosphere, causing mass panic. Everyone inside the gate got as low as they could to the earth. Even J-Fool, who was strapped, was forced to take cover behind a parked SUV. When the shots stopped, J-Fool peeked around the truck and noticed a box Chevy kicking up dust. He raised his gun to return shots, but figured he'd just be wasting bullets since the Chevy was too far away. Khalil and Janay made their way out of the gate and found J-Fool standing over Pimp. When Khalil walked up on Pimp, tears instantly cascaded down both sides of his face. Pimp was slumped with his knees tucked up under him, and his face buried in the pavement resembling a Muslim making salat.

"It was too late when I got here, fam," J-Fool explained. Khalil kneeled, then rolled Pimp over and as clear as day he was dead, with holes in him the size of hockey pucks. Janay placed a hand on Khalil's back and began to rub him tenderly.

"I'm sorry, Khalil," she proclaimed with lamentation. Khalil grabbed Pimp's phone, money, and keys from his pocket, then stood up.

"Go get the car, Janay," Khalil demanded. Janay did as she was told.

"These niggaz over here wanna fuck wit' the gang? I'm finna kill every mothafucka that come out this gate," Khalil threatened through clenched teeth, tears still leaking from his eyes.

"Hold up, fam," J-Fool suggested. "You know we gone stand on big bidness. Just not right nah, fam," J-Fool said, tucking his pistol in hand. “Them niggaz in that Chevy all had Haitian flags, fam,” J-Fool explained.

Seconds later, Janay pulled up in the whip. Even though they knew Pimp was dead, J-Fool and Khalil loaded him in the car and took him to the hospital.

* * *

Khalil had gone through Pimp’s phone and found his sister’s contact number. He convinced her to meet him and Janay at the Jetty and gave her the money for Pimp’s burial.

“Thank you, Khalil. You really meant a lot to my brother,” Teka expressed. Khalil’s expression turned quizzical. “Yeah, my brother used to talk about’chu all the time. He used to tell me that you was his lil brother,” she continued to explain. A tear fell from Khalil’s right eye, but he quickly swiped it away.

“You know, my father went to prison for life when I was younger. Pimp took me under his wing, so to me he was like a father figure,” Khalil voiced emotionally. Teka nodded her head in understanding.

“Listen, I don’t want a funeral for my brother. I prefer to have him cremated.” Khalil nodded with understanding. “I’ll get’chu an urn, so that we can both have a part of him,” said Teka.

“Okay, thank you.”

“No problem.”

“I got the keys to Pimp’s house, if you want any of his belongings,” Khalil remarked.

“No, I’m good, honey. You can keep whatever you want,” Teka responded, standing to leave. Khalil stood too. “It was nice meeting you. You have my number, call me anytime,” Teka offered, hugging Khalil.

“Fasho,” he replied before she walked off. Moments later, Janay approached. She had been standing off to the side, while Teka and Khalil had a sit down at Hurricane's outside bar.

"Everything okay?" Janay asked, hugging and kissing Khalil.

"Yeah, everything G," Khalil assured. Janay unwrapped her arms from around Khalil and stood pigeon toed with her hand on her hips.

"You found out who hit Pimp yet?" she asked.

"I gotta idea who it was," he responded. Janay looked off to the side for a moment, then diverted her attention back to Khalil.

"Wassup?" he asked.

"Khalil, I gotta tell you somethin'."

Chapter 32
(I Love You Man)

A week later…

"I know why the caged bird sings / Maya Angelou
I just did fifteen / for a bliky and some phantom dope
I attempted murda in the first / Let the hammer blow
tried to kill dem country ass niggaz / Barry Manalo
Barry Manalo? / Yeeeaaa… Barry Manalo
Ask a bitch / I'm known to act a donkey / on the cameltoe."

The sounds of "Big Khufu" blared inside the BMW that Khalil had rented for the weekend. He was headed to a foreclosed home that Janay found for them to trap out of. While Khalil was in deep thought, Kaleb reached and turned the music down.

"Bra, who this nigga is?" asked Kaleb.

"That's that nigga big Khufu Da Blazer," Khalil stated.

"Da Blazer?"

"Yeah, he Rollack! He be wit' that nigga Ola Ken outta Summer Hill, Georgia."

"Rollack?" Kaleb asked, confused.

"Yeah, they Bloods. Big Khufu from Fort Pierce, though," Khalil added.

"He from the city? Yeah, he slidin'!" Khalil nodded his head in agreement.

"So, where we goin'?" Kaleb asked. Khalil inhaled and exhaled deeply.

"When Pimp got killed, I realized that family is all we got. If I'ma be out here in these trenches, I might as well surround myself wit family," Khalil explained. "You asked me to put'chu on, so that's what I'ma do."

"Fareal?" Kaleb asked excitedly.

“Yeah! Just know that this life come wit’ a lot,” Khalil warned.

“I know what time it is. I’m ready, bra,” Kaleb assured.

“I hear you. bra,” Khalil replied.

* * *

Khalil turned right on Orleander then made a left on Azzurier. He then pulled into the fifth house on the right and put the car in park.

“Look in the console,” Khalil proclaimed mildly. When Kaleb opened the console, it was an ounce of heroin and a few thousand dollars. Kaleb pocketed the money then grabbed the dope, examining it.

“What this is?”

“That’s heroin,” Khalil explained.

“I’on know ‘bout no heroin.”

“Put that shit in ya pocket. I’ma show you how to sack it up when we get inside,” Khalil declared, hopping out of the BMW.

Kaleb put the dope in his pocket then followed behind his brother. When Kaleb entered the home, he noted that it wasn’t furnished at all.

“Damn, bra! This shit empty!” Kaleb stated, looking around.

“Yeah, but wait till I get it decorated,” Khalil pronounced, putting a pair of latex gloves on.

“Why you puttin’ gloves on?” Kaleb asked.

“You can’t touch that heroin. You gotta suck it up with gloves, or it will get in ya system.”

“Oh, okay,” Kaleb retorted.

“Put the shit on the kitchen counter,” Khalil sputtered, making his way in the kitchen and standing by the counter.

“Where my gloves at?” Kaleb asked, putting the dope on the counter.

"In that cabinet, right there," Khalil said. Kaleb reached for the cabinet.

"Fuck nigga!" Khalil yelled, jamming a hunting knife into Kaleb's armpit.

"Aaahh!" Kaleb cried.

"Shut the fuck up, nigga. Bitch ass nigga," Khalil snapped, twisting the knife every time he plunged it deep into his brother's flesh.

Khalil hit Kaleb all in his side and back multiple times, until he fell face forward. Khalil turned Kaleb on his back and looked him in the eyes, while he continued to stab him in the chest and stomach.

"I love you, bra… Khalil, I love you, man," Kaleb cried while getting stabbed. Khalil placed his left hand over Kaleb's mouth.

"Shut the fuck up, nigga," Khalil barked through clenched teeth and proceeded to stab Kaleb until his soul left his body.

After putting the knife, gloves, and all his clothes in a trash bag, Khalil headed to the back room where he had a change of clothes. He changed clothes, then called Janay from a burner phone.

"Wassup, daddy?" Janay answered. "Yeah, I'm pullin' in right nah," she retorted.

"Aight." Click! Khalil hung the phone up and headed to the kitchen. Moments later, Janay walked in with J-Fool behind her.

"In here!" Khalil called out. Janay and J-Fool made their way to the kitchen.

"What the fuck?" J-Fool asked, confused.

"You okay, daddy?" Janay asked, glancing at Kaleb's twisted body, then back at Khalil.

"Yeah, I'm good," he assured.

"That's yo' brother?" J-Fool questioned.

"Yeah," Khalil answered.

"What happened, fam?"

"Kaleb the one who shot'chu," Khalil explained to J-Fool.

"What? How you know that, fam?"

"Janay was looking outta the window, when he caught'chu wit'cha back turnt."

"Hold up, fam. I'm confused. Why would yo' brother shoot me?"

"Kaleb was jealous kuz I gave you work. He asked me to put him on, I told him no. You know the rest," Khalil pronounced, leaving the real reason he killed Kaleb out. Khalil was mad that Kaleb had shot J-Fool, but the real reason he killed his own brother was because of Pimp. Khalil felt that if it wasn't for Kaleb asking Pimp to attend his football game, Pimp would still be alive. Khalil was dead wrong. Pimp was already marked for death once he robbed Haitian Gerby.

"Damn, fam! You killed yo' own brother for me?" J-Fool asked.

"Nigga, you my brother too! We bonded by murda! Anybody that transgresses against F.S.G. getting' slaughtered," Khalil declared.

"Real shit!" Janay added.

"Listen. If you woulda found out that my brother shot'chu, you would of killed'em. That's my brother, he violated, so I dealt wit' it. I'd expect you to do the same, if it was the other way around," Khalil enunciated.

"Fasho, fam," J-Fool assured, but secretly felt ambivalent about the situation. In J-Fool's mind, he would ride with his brother, no matter if he was right or wrong. *This nigga killed his own brother. I gotta watch this nigga. Then Janay gotta nerve to be wit' this nigga. I gotta watch her too*, J-Fool thought.

Chapter 33
(I'm Hit)

"Hey, daddy. I'm just callin' you to check on you. I heard about Pimp. You okay?" Erica asked.

"That shit fucked me up, but I'ma be aight. One day at a time," Khalil replied.

"Okay, well, I'm here if you wanna get away or just talk. Call me," Erica enunciated.

"Fasho." Moments later, Penny walked into Khalil's old room.

"Look, I'ma call you later," said Khalil.

"Okay, daddy," Erica replied, hanging up.

"Wassup, Moma? You aight?" Khali asked, sitting up to spark a blunt.

"No. Yo' brother didn't come home last night. You seen him?" Penny asked.

"I ain't seen him, Moma. What about Pimp? How you dealin' wit' that?" Penny shrugged her shoulders.

"You know me and Pimp was just friends. He had other women, so wasn't no real love there. We just used to fuck," Penny admitted.

"Come on, Ma!" Khalil muttered.

"What? I'm just keeping shit real. Pimp was in them streets, anyway. I knew it was gone catch up wit'em one day. Let me hit that blunt," Penny asked, reaching for the weed. Khalil took a pull then handed it to her. She inhaled deeply, then exhaled.

"All I got left is my two babies," Penny declared. Moments later, there was a knock at the door. Penny hit the blunt once more, then headed downstairs to see who was at the door.

"Ma'am, are you Ms. Penny Vaughn?" asked one of the officers.

"Yes, I am! How may I help you?"

"Sorry to inform you that we found your son Kaleb's body in a foreclosure home. He'd been stabbed to death over what appeared to be a drug deal gone wrong. I'm sorry for your loss, ma'am," the officer proclaimed then walked away with his partner in tow.

"Oh, my God! No!" Penny wailed, then collapsed in Khalil's arms. "No, not my baby!" She continued to cry and shake repetitiously. Khalil hugged and rubbed his mother's back.

"It's gone be okay, Moma," Khalil declared.

* * *

Two weeks later…

"When I'm fishin' through yo' trenches/ AMG this bitch tinted

Niggas heard I'm tryna end'em/ So they say they gone surrender

I won't tell a soul when I get-em/ Nigga know that I'ma reaper"

J-Fool sat in the passenger seat of the Genesis, listening to his favorite "Jumpman Krank" song while Janay drove, and Khalil smoked one in the back passenger seat. J-Fool turned the volume down.

"Fam, you know Jumpman Krank was from the 3, right?" J-Fool asked.

"Yeah, bra I know," Khalil retorted.

"He was a real reaper, fam! I miss my nigga, fam!" J-Fool expressed then turned the volume back up. J-Fool's reminiscence made Khalil think of Pimp. He secretly wiped tears from his face then cleared his throat.

"Aye!" he yelled. J-Fool turned the music down.

"Wassup, fam?" J-Fool asked, looking back at Khalil.

"We here, turn that off. Janay, pull over right here, cut the lights," Khalil quarterbacked. It was three in the morning without a soul in sight.

"Drop them ski's, let's go. Janay, grab the can," Khalil ordered.

All three of them pulled their ski masks down. Khalil and J-Fool grabbed their MAC 90's while Janay grabbed the gas can and made their way in front of Gerby's house. Janay started at the front right side of the house pouring gas, and made her way around the left side and round back. Khalil and J-Fool made their way around the right side and squatted by Gerby's window. When Janay made her way to Khalil and J-Fool, she sat the can down and pulled a lighter from her pocket.

Boc! Boc! Boc! Boc!

Four shots rang out from inside the house, one of them hitting Janay in the arm, flipping her.

"Aaah! Sshit!" she moaned. Khalil pointed his MAC 90 in the window in the back of the house, while J-Fool pointed his in the same room in the window to the left side. They waved their weapons from side to side and emptied their clips.

"You aight, ma?" Khalil asked, reloading his MAC 90.

"Yeah," she mumbled, getting up to grab the can. J-Fool picked the lighter up then set the house ablaze. Khalil sprayed a few more rounds in the window, while J-Fool reloaded, then ran towards the front of the house to see if Gerby and his family would run out. Janay made her way to the rental and got into the backseat. Flames crawled up all sides of the house rapidly. Nobody came out, so Khalil and J-Fool sprayed the front of the house until they were empty, then ran to the car, hopped in, then pulled off.

"You good, fam?" J-Fool asked from the driver's seat.

"Yeah, I'm hit in the arm, like by my shoulder," she moaned.

"We gone dump the guns and whip, then take her to St. Mary's in Gifford. We can't go to Lawnwood," Khalil pronounced.

"Yeah, you right, fam," J-Fool assured.

"Janay, I love you," Khalil expressed.

"I love you too, daddy," Janay replied, putting pressure on her wound.

"Here y'all go wit' all this sentimental shit," J-Fool added.

Chapter 34

(Come Here)

Janay's wound was an in and out one. She was checked out of St. Mary's two hours later by her sister Latoya. Khalil and J-Fool had learned that Gerby, his baby mother Kia, and their baby boy had all died in the fire. The reason that no one ran out of the burning house was because Gerby and Kia and suffered gunshot wounds, and the baby boy had simply burned to death. Khalil knew that Pimp had robbed some Haitians on Mayflower Street but didn't know that he'd gunned Gerby and Kia down, and that they had survived. He was now laid up with Janay tending to her every need.

"Who keep callin' yo' phone?" Janay asked. Khalil sent the caller to voicemail for the fourth time.

"Marcia," he answered.

"Why you won't answer? Next time she call, let me answer the phone," Janay proclaimed. Seconds later, Marcia was calling again.

"Here," Khalil said, handing Janay the phone. She answered, putting it on speaker.

"Hello?" Janay answered seductively.

"Umm… may I please speak to Khalil?" Marcia asked.

"Who is this?" Janay asked, already knowing.

"Marcia! Who is this?" Marcia replied.

"Marcia, girl, this is Janay. I been meaning to talk to you about something, girl."

"Girl, bye! What me and you got to talk about? We not friends! Just put Khalil on the phone, please," Marcia pleaded.

"See, that's what I wanted to talk to you about."

"What?" Marcia snapped.

"Listen, we ain't gotta have no tension 'bout Khalil. It's plenty of room in this California for you too," Janay proposed. Click! Marcia hung the phone up. Khalil laughed.

"You a trip," Khalil stated, placing a kiss on Janay's big soft lips.

"I'm graveyard serious! She gone have to get wit' it or get lost. I'll give her a lil time to ponder my offer," added Janay.

"Oh yeah?"

"Yeah," Janay assured.

"Ponder this," Khalil retorted, rolling on top of her and kissing her aggressively. Janay obliged, kissing him back while moaning. Khalil kissed on her neck, leaving a trail of wetness as he made his way to her perfect mango-sized breasts. Khalil's dick throbbed simultaneously with the heat that flooded between her legs.

"Fffuck, daddy," Janay whispered, moving her pussy in a slow circular motion while Khalil made his way down her stomach.

"Talk to me," he said just above a whisper, in between kisses.

"I wont'chu too—" Janay inhaled quickly. "Ooowe, daddy!" She cried gripping the sheets when Khalil came in contact with her clit.

"Mmm-hmm!" Khalil taunted, sucking on her clit not too hard but with just the right amount of pressure. He switched the method up and began to flick his tongue rapidly, barely touching her clit.

"Ssss, whoooo…, I fuckin' love you!" Janay screamed. Khalil flattened his tongue, moved it from left to right, up and down, sucked her clit for a moment, then blew softly. This technique caused Janay to squirt. Her nectar shot out like a spout, hitting Khalil directly in the face.

"Ssss… whoooooo…, I… um so… sss… sorry, daddy," Janay apologized, trembling.

"Fuck! I love that shit," Khalil admitted licking his lips, then rising to his knees. He grabbed Janay's petite frame, then flipped her on her stomach.

"Mmm!" Janay moaned, turned on by his aggressiveness. He pushed her left leg up at an angle leaving her right leg straight, then slid in her from behind.

"Ummmm," they both moaned in unison. Khalil used both hands to grip her left ass cheek, then began to stroke her long, slow, and deep.

"Sss… ooow, that dick good," she cried, arching her back a little so that he could hit her bottom. Within two minutes, Janay was squirting all over Khalil, soaking him from the waist down. Her warm juices and pussy spasms caused him to pick up his pace, gripping her soft cheeks and fucking her violently. Clap! Clap! Clap! Clap! Clap! Janay's ass cheeks jiggled beautifully to a divine rhythm.

"Hhhaa! Sss… whoo, fuck me!" Janay screamed through clenched teeth.

"Come here! Huh? Take it! Sss… fffuck! That's it! Take this dick," Khalil growled, shooting all of his semen deep inside Janay's canal.

"Sss… whooo… yes! Nut all in this pussy, daddy!" Janay cried, cumming with Khalil.

"Fuck, bitch… I love you!" Khalil stated, collapsing on top of Janay. Janay caught her breath before responding.

"I love yo' ass too, nigga!"

Chapter 35

Three days later…

Khalil consoled his mother while she grieved the loss of her son, Kaleb. A few family members flew in from the Bahamas, to pay their respects, and so did a few students from his school. Even Marcia attended to pay hers also. J-Fool chose to wait in the car and smoke multiple blunts. He wasn't there to pay his respect to Kaleb, due to him being the one who made an attempt on his life. The church was in Haitian territory, so he attended in the parking lot to watch Khalil's back. He also wanted to see if Khalil would really carry his brother's casket after killing him. When the church doors opened and J-Fool saw that Khalil was one of the pall bearers, he knew then that he was affiliated with a different type of breed. He noted that Khalil's expression was emotionless and came to the conclusion that Khalil was treacherous by nature. After loading the casket in the hearse, Khalil made his way towards J-Fool's whip. J-Fool dropped the window.

"Wassup fam?" J-Fool asked.

"I'm good, bra. I'm finna go wit' my ol girl to the graveyard. You can slide. I appreciate'chu holdin' me down, my nigga," Khalil remarked.

"You already know! F.S.G. type shit," J-Fool retorted.

"Listen! As soon as we leave the graveyard, I'ma hit'cha line. We gotta get the trap back bumpin'!" Khalil said, looking around and checking his surroundings.

"Fasho, fam. Just hit me," J-Fool replied.

"Yeah!" J-Fool put his car in drive then pulled off. When Khalil turned around, Marcia was approaching.

"Hey, Khalil," she greeted, wrapping her arms around Khalil

"Wassup? Appreciate'chu coming."

"No problem. How you holding up?" she asked, unwrapping her arms from around him. Khalil shrugged.

"Death is a part of life, right? From the moment we born… ain't shit promised to you, but death. So, yeah, I'm aight," he assured.

"I guess that's a way of looking at it. Where's Janay?"

"I told her not to come. Why?"

"Just asking," Marcia chimed.

"Khalil! Come on, let's go!" Penny called out.

"I'ma catch you later," Khalil proclaimed, kissing Marcia on the lips.

"Okay, baby," she retorted, watching Khalil get into his truck and take off with his mother.

* * *

After watching his brother get lowered into the ground, Khalil offered to take his mother out to eat, but she politely declined. She gazed out of the window, trying to wrap her head around Kaleb dying over a drug deal.

"Somethin' ain't right," Penny voiced, her leg shaking.

"What'chu mean?" Khalil asked.

"Kaleb was a good boy. He wouldn't sell no drugs." Penny turned and gazed at Khalil. "Khalil, did you give your brother drugs?"

"Nawl, Moma. I wouldn't do that, knowing he wanted to pursue football," lied Khalil.

"The shit just don't make sense. Where is you going?" asked Penny.

"I gotta stop by Pimp's house to grab somethin'. That's cool wit'chu?" Penny inhaled, then exhaled deeply.

"I guess. You gotta joint?"

"Yeah, look in the console."

"You got some molly?"

"Nawl, I'm not givin you no molly!" Penny sucked her teeth.

"Whateva," she replied sparking the blunt. Moments later, Khalil pulled into Pimp's home that was down the street from the one he had burned down.

"So, this where that nigga lived? He ain't never brought me here! I'm finna come in wit'chu!" Penny claimed.

"Nawl! It's too dangerous over here! Stay yo' ass in the truck! I'll be right back. Blow the horn if you see somethin'."

"What the hell blowin' the horn gone do?" she clowned, taking a pull from the blunt.

"It's a pistol under my seat," Khalil stated, getting out and heading inside. Khalil headed straight to Pimp's room. He flipped the bed, went through drawers, and his closet. After the search was done, Khalil had two old Russian AK's, four handguns, five bricks of heroin, and over one hundred fifty thousand in cash. He loaded everything into two duffle bags and took them to his truck, placing them in the back seat.

"Boy, what's all that?" questioned Penny. Khalil closed the back door then hopped in the front seat.

"All this gone change our life," he retorted, putting the truck in reverse then pulling off.

"Change our life?"

"Yeah, I'm moving you outta that Section 8 shit. I'ma get'chu a house." Penny chuckled.

"After what I been through, you really think that's gone make me happy?"

"Nawl, but it'll make me happy knowing I did it. Too many traumatizing memories in that apartment," Khalil voiced.

"Well, I guess you my damn daddy nah, huh?" Penny implied, still smoking a blunt. Khalil's phone began to ring as soon as he made it across Okeechobee Road.

"Yeah, wassup?" he answered.

"I'm just checkin' on you," Janay stated.

"Fasho, I'm good. I got my moma in the truck wit' me. We finna handle a lil bidness, then I'ma call you back," Khalil proclaimed.

"Okay, daddy. Love you."

"Love you, too," he replied then hung up.

"Love you? Well, damn! When I'ma get to meet her?" Penny asked.

"Soon," Khalil promised, making a right on 23rd Street. Seconds later, Khalil noted a detective on his bumper. Moments later, the unmarked car cut on its lights.

"Fuck!" Khalil yelled.

"What?"

"Them krackaz behind me!" Penny turned to look.

"What all you got in them bags?"

"Tsss… dope, guns, and money," he explained. Penny took a deep breath then exhaled.

"Pull over, I'ma say it's mines," Penny suggested.

"Fuck no! I'm in a fuckin Aston Martin! They won't catch me," Khalil said with assurance.

"And what if you wreck out and kill us both? Fuck no! Look, I don't care about nothin' no more! You all I got! So, pull the fuck over, and I'ma say the shit is mines!"

"Nawl, we ain't doin' that!" Penny gazed at Khalil, then quickly stretched her left leg on Khalil's side and pressed the brake. Both of their bodies jerked forward. Penny grabbed the steering wheel tightly and wouldn't release it.

"You trippin!" Khalil mentioned, watching the unmarked car cut them off. Another one pulled behind him and jumped out with guns drawn.

"Get the fuck out! On the ground now!" both officers yelled.

***

An hour later…

Khalil was in the interrogation room waiting to hear the spiel the detective was going to lay out. After what seemed like an eternity, the detective finally came in with a Coke soda and some sour cream and onion chips.

"You look hungry. Soda? Chips?" he offered.

"Maan, why the fuck you pulled me over?" Khalil snapped. The detective chuckled.

"You wanna hear something funny?"

"Yeah, tell me what the fuck is so funny," Khalil sneered.

"I wasn't pulling you. I cut my lights on for you to pull aside and let me by. I had a call up the street, but when you didn't pull over and stopped abruptly… I told myself… I said, 'Self… you might wanna check that Aston Martin out.' Then, I'll be damned… Jackpot!" the detective pronounced excitedly. Khalil shook his head in disappointment.

"Where my moma?"

"Well, yo' moma is in another room claiming everything is hers, but I know that's bullshit."

"What makes you call bullshit?"

"We wasn't after you today, but your name been coming across me desk lately, Khalil. Or shall I say, Killa!" the detective pronounced with a smile. *Da fuck*, Khalil thought.

"Before your brother was killed, he had a lot to say and I think you know what I'm touching on," the detective said, interlocking his fingers.

"I don't know what'chu speakin' on… Detective…?"

"Pearson! Kevin Pearson, and listen. I don't give a fuck if you YN's kill each other. That's one less body me and my guys don't have to drop. You feel me… homie?"

"Fuck you!" Khalil spat.

"I'm tired of playing with you! Here's how it's going to be! You're going to tell me where you got that dope and them guns, or you and your mother will never see the streets again!" Pearson threatened.

"Suck my dick!" Khalil barked.

"You'll have plenty of men to do that for you in prison! I'm done talking!" Pearson proclaimed, standing to leave.

"Wait!" Khalil pronounced.

"What?" Pearson questioned.
"What about my money?"

To Be Continued…

Treacherous YN 2
(A Thin Line Between Loyalty and Betrayal)

Coming Soon!!!

Lock Down Publications and Ca$h Presents Assisted Publishing Packages

Due to an increase in the price of services we have increased our prices. The prices below reflect the price increase as of 11/1/24.

BASIC PACKAGE **$699** Editing Cover Design Formatting	**UPGRADED PACKAGE** **$1000** Typing Editing Cover Design Formatting Upload eBooks to Amazon Upload Paperback to Amazon
ADVANCE PACKAGE **$1,400** Typing Editing (line editing/content) Cover Design Formatting Copyright Registration Proofreading Upload eBooks to Amazon Upload Paperback to Amazon	**LDP SUPREME PACKAGE** **$1,700** Typing Editing (line editing/content) Cover Design Formatting Copyright Registration Proofreading Set up Amazon Account Upload eBooks to Amazon Upload Paperback to Amazon Advertise on LDP's Amazon and Facebook Page

***

Other services available upon request.
Additional charges may apply

Lock Down Publications
P.O. Box 944
Stockbridge, GA 30281-9998
Phone: 470 303-9761
Email: lockdownpublications@gmail.com

Submission Guideline

Submit the first three chapters of your completed manuscript to ldpsubmissions@gmail.com. In the subject line add **Your Book's Title**. The manuscript must be in a Word Doc file and sent as an attachment. Document should be in Times New Roman, double spaced, and in size 12 font. Also, provide your synopsis and full contact information. If sending multiple submissions, they must each be in a separate email.

Have a story but no way to send it electronically? You can still submit to LDP/Ca$h Presents. Send in the first three chapters, written or typed, of your completed manuscript to:

LDP: Submissions Dept
P.O. Box 944
Stockbridge, GA 30281-9998

DO NOT send original manuscript. Must be a duplicate. Provide your synopsis and a cover letter containing your full contact information.

Thanks for considering LDP and Ca$h Presents.

NEW RELEASES

BLOODLINE OF A SAVAGE 1-3
THESE VICIOUS STREETS 1-3
RELENTLESS GOON 1-3
SOULLESS GOON 1&2
BY PRINCE A. TAUHID

THE BUTTERFLY MAFIA 3
BY FUMIYA PAYNE

A THUG'S STREET PRINCESS 1&2
BY MEESHA

CITY OF SMOKE 1-3
BY MOLOTTI

GET IT IN SLUGS 1 &2
BY B. STALL

STANDING ON HER BUSINESS 1&2
BY DG SANTANA

STEPPERS 1,2&3
THE REAL BADDIES OF CHI-RAQ 1-3
BY KING RIO

THE LANE 1-3
BY KEN-KEN SPENCE

THUG OF SPADES 1&2
LOVE IN THE TRENCHES 1&2
CORNER BOYS 1&2
ONCE YOU GO GANGSTA
PROTÉGÉ OF A LEGEND 1- 3
BY COREY ROBINSON

TIL DEATH 3
BY ARYANNA

THE BIRTH OF A GANGSTER 4
BY DELMONT PLAYER

PRODUCT OF THE STREETS 1-3
BY DEMOND "MONEY" ANDERSON

MONEY HUNGRY DEMONS 1-2
BY TRANAY ADAMS

TRAP STARS
BY B. SHELLY

HUB CITY MENACE 1-4
BY J. WHITE

A THUGGISH PASSION 1&2
LAND OF DA HOOLIGANZ 1-4
KILLAZ ON STANDBY 1&2
FRESH OFF DA PORCH 1-3
SECURE DA BAG
AMBITIONS OF A SLIDER
FOR MY ENEMIES SAKE
SOULLESS GOON 1&2
FO'EVA ROLLIN 1-4
BY ASSA RAYMOND BAKER

THE LEVEL UP 1&2
BY LUXURY KING

HUNGRY FOR MONEY 1&2
SLIMBOS

QUEEN OF NAPTOWN 1&2
THA TAKEOVER 1-3
BY KEITH CHANDLER

DRILL CITY 1&2
BY ZAY'TOWVEN

LOVE ME OR LET ME GO
BY R. FACEY

SAVAGE DREAMZ
BY KING DAVID

MONEY AND DEAD HOMIES
BY DERRICK SUMMERS

WHITE BOYS
BY BANDEMIC

A THUGS STREET PRINCESS 3 Coming Soon
BY MEESHA

BETRAYAL OF A G 2
BY RAY VINCI

SAVAGE FAMILY EMPIRE 1&2
SOULLESS GOON 1&2
THE DIRTY SIDE OF MONEY 1,2&3
BY PRINCE

BY THE TRUCKLOAD 1-4 COMING SOON
T SOULLESS GOON 1&2
IPPIN' THE SCALES 1-4
BAD BITCHES WIT GUNZ 1-3
PROBLEM SOLVED 1-3
THE GIRLRILLA AND HER N*GGA
THE SINGLE LADIES
BY CHRISTOPHER "DIESEL" HORNEZES

AVAILABLE NOW

RESTRAINING ORDER 1 & 2
BY CA$H & COFFEE

LOVE KNOWS NO BOUNDARIES 1-3
BY COFFEE

RAISED AS A GOON I, II, III & IV
BRED BY THE SLUMS I, II, III
BLAST FOR ME I & II
ROTTEN TO THE CORE I II III
A BRONX TALE I, II, III
DUFFLE BAG CARTEL I II III IV V VI
HEARTLESS GOON I II III IV V
A SAVAGE DOPEBOY I II
DRUG LORDS I II III
CUTTHROAT MAFIA I II
KING OF THE TRENCHES
BY GHOST

LAY IT DOWN I & II
LAST OF A DYING BREED I II
BLOOD STAINS OF A SHOTTA I & II III
BY JAMAICA

LOYAL TO THE GAME I II III
LIFE OF SIN I, II III
BY TJ & JELISSA

IF LOVING HIM IS WRONG…I & II
LOVE ME EVEN WHEN IT HURTS I II III
BY JELISSA

PUSH IT TO THE LIMIT
BY BRE' HAYES

TREACHEROUS YN | KHUFU

BLOODY COMMAS I & II
SKI MASK CARTEL I, II & III
KING OF NEW YORK I II, III IV V
RISE TO POWER I II III
COKE KINGS I II III IV V
BORN HEARTLESS I II III IV
KING OF THE TRAP I II
BY T.J. EDWARDS

WHEN THE STREETS CLAP BACK I & II III
THE HEART OF A SAVAGE I II III IV
MONEY MAFIA I II
LOYAL TO THE SOIL I II III
BY JIBRIL WILLIAMS

A DISTINGUISHED THUG STOLE MY HEART I II & III
LOVE SHOULDN'T HURT I II III IV
RENEGADE BOYS 1-4
PAID IN KARMA 1-3
SAVAGE STORMS 1-3
AN UNFORESEEN LOVE 1-3
BABY, I'M WINTERTIME COLD 1-3
A THUG'S STREET PRINCESS 1,2&3
EMBRACING THE LOVE OF A BOSS
BY MEESHA

A GANGSTER'S CODE 1-3
A GANGSTER'S SYN 1-3
THE SAVAGE LIFE 1-3
CHAINED TO THE STREETS 1-3
BLOOD ON THE MONEY 1-3
A GANGSTA'S PAIN 1-3
BEAUTIFUL LIES AND UGLY TRUTHS
CHURCH IN THESE STREETS
BY J-BLUNT

CUM FOR ME 1-8
AN LDP EROTICA COLLABORATION

TREACHEROUS YN | KHUFU

BLOOD OF A BOSS 1-5
SHADOWS OF THE GAME
TRAP BASTARD
BY ASKARI

THE STREETS BLEED MURDER 1-3
THE HEART OF A GANGSTA 1-3
BY JERRY JACKSON

WHEN A GOOD GIRL GOES BAD
BY ADRIENNE

THE COST OF LOYALTY 1-3
BY KWELI

BRIDE OF A HUSTLA 1-3
THE FETTI GIRLS 1-3
CORRUPTED BY A GANGSTA 1-4
BLINDED BY HIS LOVE
THE PRICE YOU PAY FOR LOVE 1-3
DOPE GIRL MAGIC 1-3
BY DESTINY SKAI

A KINGPIN'S AMBITION
A KINGPIN'S AMBITION II
I MURDER FOR THE DOUGH
BY AMBITIOUS

TRUE SAVAGE 1-7
DOPE BOY MAGIC 1-3
MIDNIGHT CARTEL 1-3
CITY OF KINGZ 1&2
NIGHTMARE ON SILENT AVE
THE PLUG OF LIL MEXICO 1&2
CLASSIC CITY
BY CHRIS GREEN

GANGSTA CITY
BY TEDDY DUKE

BACK IN BLOOD
SEX, MURDER AND GOD 1&2
COUNTDOWN OF A KILLA 1&2
GUNS DOWN, BOTTOMS UP 1&2
BY LO-LIFE

A GANGSTER'S REVENGE 1-4
THE BOSS MAN'S DAUGHTERS 1-5
A SAVAGE LOVE 1&2
BAE BELONGS TO ME 1&2
A HUSTLER'S DECEIT 1-3
WHAT BAD BITCHES DO 1-3
SOUL OF A MONSTER 1-3
KILL ZONE
A DOPE BOY'S QUEEN 1-3
TIL DEATH 1-3
IMMA DIE BOUT MINE 1-6
DYING FOR LIKES 1&2
KILLA CREW 1&2
BY ARYANNA

A DOPEBOY'S PRAYER
BY EDDIE "WOLF" LEE

THE KING CARTEL 1-3
BY FRANK GRESHAM

THESE NIGGAS AIN'T LOYAL 1-3
BY NIKKI TEE

GANGSTA SHYT 1-3
BY CATO

THE ULTIMATE BETRAYAL
BY PHOENIX

BOSS'N UP 1-3
BY ROYAL NICOLE

I LOVE YOU TO DEATH
BY DESTINY J

I RIDE FOR MY HITTA
I STILL RIDE FOR MY HITTA
BY MISTY HOLT

LOVE & CHASIN' PAPER
BY QAY CROCKETT

TO DIE IN VAIN
SINS OF A HUSTLA
BY ASAD

BROOKLYN HUSTLAZ
BY BOOGSY MORINA

A DRUG KING AND HIS DIAMOND 1-3
A DOPEMAN'S RICHES
HER MAN, MINE'S TOO 1&2
CASH MONEY HO'S
THE WIFEY I USED TO BE 1&2
PRETTY GIRLS DO NASTY THINGS
BY NICOLE GOOSBY

LIPSTICK KILLAH 1-3
CRIME OF PASSION 1-3
FRIEND OR FOE 1-3
BY MIMI

TRAPHOUSE KING 1-3
KINGPIN KILLAZ 1-3
STREET KINGS 1&2
PAID IN BLOOD 1&2
CARTEL KILLAZ 1-3
DOPE GODS 1&2
BY HOOD RICH

BROOKLYN ON LOCK 1 & 2
BY SONOVIA

THE STREETS ARE CALLING
BY DUQUIE WILSON

STEADY MOBBN' 1-3
THE STREETS STAINED MY SOUL 1-3
BY MARCELLUS ALLEN

WHO SHOT YA 1-3
SON OF A DOPE FIEND 1-4
HEAVEN GOT A GHETTO 1&2
SKI MASK MONEY 1&2
BY RENTA

GORILLAZ IN THE BAY 1-4
TEARS OF A GANGSTA 1/&2
3X KRAZY 1&2
STRAIGHT BEAST MODE 1&2
BY DE'KARI

SLAUGHTER GANG 1-3
RUTHLESS HEART 1-3
BY WILLIE SLAUGHTER

GOD BLESS THE TRAPPERS 1-3
THESE SCANDALOUS STREETS 1-3
FEAR MY GANGSTA 1-5
THESE STREETS DON'T LOVE NOBODY 1-2
BURY ME A G 1-5
A GANGSTA'S EMPIRE 1-4
THE DOPEMAN'S BODYGAURD 1&2
THE REALEST KILLAZ 1-3
THE LAST OF THE OGS 1-3
BY TRANAY ADAMS

MARRIED TO A BOSS 1-3
BY DESTINY SKAI & CHRIS GREEN

TRIGGADALE 1-3
MURDA WAS THE CASE 1-3
BY ELIJAH R. FREEMAN

KINGZ OF THE GAME 1-7
CRIME BOSS 1-4
BY PLAYA RAY

FUK SHYT
BY BLAKK DIAMOND

DON'T F#CK WITH MY HEART 1&2
BY LINNEA

ADDICTED TO THE DRAMA 1-3
IN THE ARM OF HIS BOSS
BY JAMILA

YAYO 1-4
A SHOOTER'S AMBITION 1&2
BRED IN THE GAME
BY S. ALLEN

TRAP GOD 1-3
RICH $AVAGE 1-3
MONEY IN THE GRAVE 1-3
CARTEL MONEY 1&2
BY MARTELL TROUBLESOME BOLDEN

FOREVER GANGSTA 1&2
GLOCKS ON SATIN SHEETS 1&2
BY ADRIAN DULAN

TOE TAGZ 1-4
LEVELS TO THIS SHYT 1&2
IT'S JUST ME AND YOU
BY AH'MILLION

LOYALTY AIN'T PROMISED 1&2
BY KEITH WILLIAMS

KINGPIN DREAMS 1-3
RAN OFF ON DA PLUG
BY PAPER BOI RARI

THE STREETS MADE ME 1-3
BY LARRY D. WRIGHT

CONFESSIONS OF A GANGSTA 1-4
CONFESSIONS OF A JACKBOY 1-3
CONFESSIONS OF A HITMAN
CONFESSIONS OF A DOPE BOY
BY NICHOLAS LOCK

I'M NOTHING WITHOUT HIS LOVE
SINS OF A THUG
TO THE THUG I LOVED BEFORE
A GANGSTA SAVED XMAS
IN A HUSTLER I TRUST
BY MONET DRAGUN

QUIET MONEY 1-3
THUG LIFE 1-3
EXTENDED CLIP 1&2
A GANGSTA'S PARADISE
BY TRAI'QUAN

CAUGHT UP IN THE LIFE 1-3
THE STREETS NEVER LET GO 1-3
BY ROBERT BAPTISTE

NEW TO THE GAME 1-3
MONEY, MURDER & MEMORIES 1-3
BY MALIK D. RICE

CREAM 2-3
THE STREETS WILL TALK
BY YOLANDA MOORE

THE STREETS WILL NEVER CLOSE 1-3
BY K'AJJI

LIFE OF A SAVAGE 1-4
A GANGSTA'S QUR'AN 1-4
MURDA SEASON 1-3
GANGLAND CARTEL 1-3
CHI'RAQ GANGSTAS 1-4
KILLERS ON ELM STREET 1-3
JACK BOYZ N DA BRONX 1-3
A DOPEBOY'S DREAM 1-3
JACK BOYS VS DOPE BOYS 1-3
COKE GIRLZ
COKE BOYS
SOSA GANG 1&2
BRONX SAVAGES
BODYMORE KINGPINS
BLOOD OF A GOON
BY ROMELL TUKES

CONCRETE KILLA 1-3
VICIOUS LOYALTY 1-3
BLOODY MONEY BAGS
BY KINGPEN

THE ULTIMATE SACRIFICE 1-6
KHADIFI
IF YOU CROSS ME ONCE 1-3
ANGEL 1-4
IN THE BLINK OF AN EYE
BY ANTHONY FIELDS

THE LIFE OF A HOOD STAR
BY CA$H & RASHIA WILSON

NIGHTMARES OF A HUSTLA 1-3
BLOOD AND GAMES 1&2
BY KING DREAM

HARD AND RUTHLESS 1&2
MOB TOWN 251
THE BILLIONAIRE BENTLEYS 1-3
REAL G'S MOVE IN SILENCE
BY VON DIESEL

MOB TIES 1-7
SOUL OF A HUSTLER, HEART OF A KILLER 1-3
GORILLAZ IN THE TRENCHES
OOPS CRY TOO 1-3
THE DAUGHTER OF A CARTEL BOSS 1&2
BY SAYNOMORE

BODYMORE MURDERLAND 1-3
THE BIRTH OF A GANGSTER 1-4
BY DELMONT PLAYER

FOR THE LOVE OF A BOSS 1&2
BY C. D. BLUE

KILLA KOUNTY 1-5
TENDER 1&2
BY KHUFU

MOBBED UP 1-4
THE BRICK MAN 1-5
THE COCAINE PRINCESS 1-10
STEPPERS 1-3
SUPER GREMLIN 1-5
A GANGSTA'S SON
THE CONNECT'S SECRET
BY KING RIO

MONEY GAME 1&2
BY SMOOVE DOLLA

TREACHEROUS YN | KHUFU

A GANGSTA'S KARMA 1-5
BY FLAME

KING OF THE TRENCHES 1-3
By GHOST & TRANAY ADAMS

QUEEN OF THE ZOO 1&2
BY BLACK MIGO

GRIMEY WAYS 1-3
BETRAYAL OF A G
BY RAY VINCI

XMAS WITH AN ATL SHOOTER
BY CA$H & DESTINY SKAI

KING KILLA 1&2
PAPER, ROCK, SNAKES
BY VINCENT "VITTO" HOLLOWAY

BETRAYAL OF A THUG 1&2
BY FRE$H

COUNTDOWN OF A KILLA 1&2
SEX, MURDER AND GOD 1&2
GUNS DOWN, BOTTOMS UP 1&2
BY LO-LIFE

FOR THE LOVE OF BLOOD 1-4
BY JAMEL MITCHELL

HOOD CONSIGLIERE 1-3
NO TIME FOR ERROR 1&2
REAL
BY KEESE

THE PLUG'S RUTHLESS DAUGHTER 1,2&3
REDEMPTION IN THE STREETS
BY TONY DANIELS

TREACHEROUS YN | KHUFU

BORN IN THE GRAVE 1-3
CRIME PAYS 1-3
BY SELF MADE TAY

MOAN IN MY MOUTH
BY XTASY

TORN BETWEEN A GANGSTER AND A GENTLEMAN
BY J-BLUNT

LOYALTY IS EVERYTHING 1-3
CITY OF SMOKE 1-3
BY MOLOTTI

HERE TODAY GONE TOMORROW 1&2
BY FLY ROCK

WOMEN LIE MEN LIE 1-4
FIFTY SHADES OF SNOW 1-3
STACK BEFORE YOU SPLURGE
GIRLS FALL LIKE DOMINOES
NAÏVE TO THE STREETS
BY ROY MILLIGAN

PILLOW PRINCESS
BY S. HAWKINS

THE BUTTERFLY MAFIA 1-3
SALUTE MY SAVAGERY 1&2
BY FUMIYA PAYNE

THE LANE 1&2
BY KEN-KEN SPENCE

THE PUSSY TRAP 1-5
BY NENE CAPRI

DIRTY DNA
BY BLAQUE

SANCTIFIED AND HORNY
BY XTASY

BOOKS BY LDP'S CEO, CA$H

TRUST IN NO MAN
TRUST IN NO MAN 2
TRUST IN NO MAN 3
BONDED BY BLOOD
SHORTY GOT A THUG
THUGS CRY
THUGS CRY 2
THUGS CRY 3
TRUST NO BITCH
TRUST NO BITCH 2
TRUST NO BITCH 3
TIL MY CASKET DROPS
RESTRAINING ORDER
RESTRAINING ORDER 2
IN LOVE WITH A CONVICT
LIFE OF A HOOD STAR
XMAS WITH AN ATL SHOOTER

www.ingramcontent.com/pod-product-compliance
Lightning Source LLC
LaVergne TN
LVHW010914110826
845149LV00013B/2363